Gideon

By

Ronna M. Bacon

ISBN 978-1-998821-35-8

Psalm 91:1-2 He who dwells in the secret place of the Most High Shall abide under the shadow of the Almighty. I will say of the Lord, "*He is* my refuge and my fortress; My God, in Him I will trust.

Psalm 62:2. He only *is* my rock and my salvation; *He is* my defense; I shall not be greatly moved.

NKJV

Table of Contents

Chapter 1

His head raising from the sermon that he was working on, Gideon Wyndsor frowned before he smiled. He could hear the youth who were practicing a song for the Sunday evening service. He rose, brushing a hand through his dark brown hair. As he walked through the church towards the sanctuary, his deep hazel eyes searched for anything that seemed out of the ordinary. A soft sound caught at his ear and he turned with a frown on his face. Seeing no one around him, Gideon shrugged and walked towards the sanctuary.

Choosing a seat about mid-way to the front, Gideon sat, a smile on his face as he listened to the chatter of the youth. His youngest brother, Gareth, was there, totally enjoying himself, he could tell. His gaze moved to one of the other leaders, a young lady around his own age. Garnet Graeme had been in town for a year or so, he thought, and had become part of the group who led the youth group.

Garnet shivered for a moment, glancing around. Her aqua-coloured eyes held fear for a moment before she tugged at the deep red-gold curls that brushed her shoulders. She felt unsafe once more. She had been on the run now for years, moving towns and employment. Garnet thought that she was safe in the town and had felt that way for months. That safety seemed to have walked away.

Gideon waited patiently as the youth passed him, high fives and hugs given. He was well loved by his congregation, and he loved them in return. He was on his feet as Gareth approached.

"Heading out of town tonight, Gareth?" Gideon eyed his brother.

"We are. Annie's folks are already at the cottage. It's not that late and the roads should be clear." Gareth hesitated. "Gideon? Are you okay?"

"I am. Why would you ask?" Gideon frowned at his brother.

Gareth shrugged. He had felt a sense of doom that night when he saw his brother. He just didn't know why. He walked away at last, not sure that he should be.

Gideon watched his brother, his frown still in place. He searched the sanctuary. The church was an old one, with pews instead of chairs. He turned to the front to find Garnet standing by the piano, staring down at it.

"Garnet?" Gideon had been quiet as he approached her, his sneakered feet not making much of a sound.

Garnet jumped, her eyes huge as she turned. A hand was on her throat as she struggled to control her emotions.

"Garnet? Are you okay?" Gideon waited for her to speak, his patience one of the qualities that endeared him to others.

Garnet was shaking with fear, struggling to control that.

“I don’t know, Gideon. Something is wrong and I don’t know what.” Garnet reached for her keys and then sighed. “Thank you for asking. Not many people bother any more.”

Gideon nodded, reaching for the portfolio that she had picked up. He did it automatically, bringing a surprised look to Garnet’s face.

“I’ll walk you out, Garnet.” A sudden sense of dread and danger had spread through him. He hesitated for a moment in the entrance to the sanctuary, feeling danger waiting.

Garnet stared at him for a moment, uncertainty in her look. A noise had her raising her head, a scream coming torn from her as a figure appeared and grabbed at her. The man caught her wrist and began to pull her away from Gideon.

Gideon gave a shout, Garnet’s portfolio dropping to the ground as he sprang towards the man. He wrenched Garnet’s wrist from the man’s tight grasp and shoved her away before he turned back to the man. He was unable to charge at the man again. The man’s knotted fist struck Gideon on his jaw, sending him backwards. Garnet’s hand on his back held him upright before he moved back into the fight.

Gideon shoved Garnet further away before he faced the man once more. They circled one another, gauging each other before the man charged at Gideon, his arms wrapping around the pastor and knocking him to the gray-tiled floor. Gideon’s breath was knocked from him and he gasped for breath as the man’s fist pounded at him. A lucky blow to his jaw again sent Gideon's head thudding to the floor where he lay still.

Garnet had watched in horror as Gideon was attacked before she ran to hide, following his shouted directions. She locked his office door behind her before her phone was in her hands and she was calling for help.

The red and blue emergency lights lit up the twilight outside of the white-sided church and reflected from the large bell in the bell tower. Officers ran for the church, one stopping beside Gideon, dropping to his knees to assess him. The church was searched for the assailant and then for Garnet. The responding officers knew that she was there. Her car was in the parking lot and her portfolio was on the floor near Gideon. James, one of the detectives on the Oak City force, paused at Gideon's door before he tried the knob. He could hear soft sounds behind it and pounded at it.

"Garnet? Are you in there?" James waited for a moment before banging once more.

Garnet jumped back for the door, terror on her face. She had not had a chance to calm herself from the sudden attack. She reached out to touch the door, not believing that help was there.

"Garnet? Open the door?" James was frustrated. He was sure that Garnet was inside the office. He turned as an officer approached and handed him Gideon's keys.

"Here. Take Gideon's keys. If Garnet is inside, she may be too scared to unlock the door." The officer stood with his back to James, monitoring the area. The assailant had not been found despite the intensive search of the church and the surrounding area.

The keys rattling in the door drove Garnet back from it. She stared at James as the door swung open, not hearing his questions to her. She ran past him, eluding his outstretched hand and headed for Gideon. She was on her knees beside him, trying to raise him into her arms despite the protests of the officers with him.

"He was hurt because of me. I don't know why. Who did this?" Garnet's glare was angry as she looked up at the officers surrounding her and then her gaze dropped back to Gideon. "He was hurt because of me and I don't know who it was. At least, I don't think that I do." Her brow furrowed as she tried to recall what the man looked like.

James' hand rested on her shoulder before he pulled her to her feet and to one side as the paramedics moved in.

"We'll talk, Garnet. Right now, are you hurt?" James watched as she rubbed at a wrist. "Did he grab you there?" He waited patiently for her to respond but her attention was solely on Gideon.

Moving her quickly to his car, James followed the ambulance to the hospital. He had put out a call to Gideon's oldest brother, Gorrie, that Gideon had been injured and was headed for help. Gorrie had been shocked to say the least, merely asking if he was alive. James could hear the relief in his voice when he responded that Gideon was. He kept shooting glances at Garnet, finding her not responsive to anything around her. He worried about her. James didn't know Garnet well, just seeing her around the church. However, it seemed as if he would get to know her better, now that she and Gideon were involved in an adventure just like others of their friends.

Garnet didn't speak, her thoughts muddled too much to make sense. She begged God to protect Gideon and heal him. She just knew that something bad would happen again and she wanted God to remove Gideon from contact with her. Garnet sighed to herself. That just wasn't going to happen, she just knew that.

Chapter 2

Walking through the Emergency Department, James headed for the room where Gideon was being assessed. Gideon had not roused at all, which worried James. He needed to talk to his pastor and friend but that didn't seem to be possible at the moment. He stood in the doorway, watching as the nurse worked to clean the blood from Gideon's face. James sighed before he walked away, looking for Gideon's family.

Gorrie stood as he saw James approaching him, an arm around their sister, Ginny. He frowned at the look on James' face.

"James?" Gorrie hugged his sister tighter. "I don't like the look on your face. What happened?"

"Have a seat, Gorrie, Ginny. We need to talk." James sat, his eyes closing for a moment. It had been a long day and was far from over. He was frustrated that another friend had been hurt coming to the aid of a beautiful lady. And he still had to track down that beautiful lady and take her statement. Garnet had not spoken to him at all since she ran from Gideon's office in the church.

"Do you have any word on him, James?" Ginny's voice held the faint trace of Ireland. All of the seven siblings did, a hangover from being raised by Irish parents who had immigrated to Canada before any of their children had been born.

"Not yet, Ginny. They're assessing him, I do believe. We'll get you back to see him." James' eyes closed for a moment as he prayed for his pastor once more. He didn't want to be here, not like this.

"What happened, James?" Gorrie spoke up, his big brother worry almost more than he could handle.

"He was attacked in the church. It looks as if he was escorting Garnet Graeme out to her car after the youth meeting. Someone attacked him. Just why, we haven't determined yet but he must have told Garnet to run. We found her locked in his office." James frowned at that. "He was unconscious when we got there."

"What has Garnet said?" Ginny knew Garnet to some degree from their ladies' Bible study group.

"She hasn't said yet, Ginny. I need to find her but I wanted to speak with you two first. Hang tight while I go back." James walked away, leaving the siblings to exchange glances before their heads were bowed and they began to pray for their brother and the lady involved.

James stood once more in Gideon's room, waiting for the physician to turn away from the bed and approach him. It was a position that he had been in many times in the past. He just had not expected it to involve his pastor. His thoughts were troubled. James would need to speak with Garnet but he wanted to speak with the physician first.

Garnet sat on the side of the stretcher, her feet dangling above the floor. She was afraid, no, terrified, she thought. She had no idea who the man had been but she had been shocked at how Gideon had stepped in to protect her. Garnet had run at his shouted commands, scrambling to find a place to hide. His office door had been open and the light on. That's why she had chosen that room, slamming the door and locking it behind her. She had backed away from the door, afraid that the man would break it down and disappear with her.

Looking down at her wrist, Garnet frowned at the bruises that were appearing. She had not realized that she had been hurt until the nurse had touched her wrist and asked her if she hurt there. Garnet had stared at her in shock, not realizing the strength of the grip that the man had had on her. Without Gideon's interference, she would not be sitting there, she now realized.

Garnet slid from the stretcher and crept to the doorway of the room. She peeked out and then almost ran for the open ambulance bay doors and through them. She reached for her phone to call for a taxi.

The taxi driver studied Garnet carefully before he nodded. He refused to let her approach her car in the church parking lot on her own.

"I'm walking over there with you, young lady. And don't protest. It's what we do in this town for ladies on their own. Now, where are your keys?" He pointed at Garnet's car. "In you get. And then I'm following you to your home." Word had spread out into the community about Gideon's attack and that he had been trying to protect Garnet. Garnet, without her knowledge, had become well known in town just from her compassion for the youth.

Garnet gave a brief nod, hitting the button on her key fob to unlock her door and slipped into the seat. Starting her vehicle, she drove off, praying for Gideon as she did so. She pleaded that he was not hurt too badly and that James would find out tonight who that man was. Garnet struggled with her emotions as she pulled up to her home and then drove into the garage. She waved at the taxi driver who had followed her. He waited until the garage door closed and lights appeared in her home. He had been worried about her. His daughter was one of the youth at the church who had been taken under Garnet's wing.

Walking through her home, Garnet rubbed at her wrist. It had not been wrapped but she reached for an ice pack and wrapped it in a towel. She folded it around her wrist, finding the cold soothing. She sighed to herself before she reached with one hand to plug in the kettle and then reach for the tea canister. Making her cup of tea, Garnet turned and headed for her bedroom. Instead, she turned to the living room, finding her favourite spot on the couch and curling up, the cup of tea on a coaster on the oak side table. Her wounded wrist was balanced on the couch arm, the ice pack firmly in place.

She was puzzled, she had to admit, before she took her puzzlement and distress to her Heavenly Father. This was how she had decided to manage her life, taking everything to her Abba Father. Her thoughts and prayers turned to Gideon. Garnet was thankful that he had stepped in. She was just worried about how hurt he might be. She had wanted to find him before she walked away but had not. She had felt driven to leave.

James stood in the examination room from where Garnet had fled. His head dropped for a moment. She just had to do that, he decided, reaching for his phone to ask for a patrol officer to swing by the church and determine if her car was still there. If it wasn't, he asked for the officer to swing by her home and determine if she was there. He would wait until morning to track her down.

Walking away from that room, James walked into Gideon's room, finding that man starting to rouse. He waited for him to awaken fully, having to leave at some point to attend another crime scene. He was frustrated at that.

Chapter 3

Early the next morning, Gideon fully roused, a hand landing on his jaw. He winced as he touched the bruise and then waggled his jaw from side to side, relieved that it was not broken. He could not remember, however, how he had been hurt.

A noise to the side of the bed caused Gideon to jump and stare that way. Fear briefly flickered through his eyes before he relaxed. Gorrie had risen to stand by the bed, his hands on the bed rail.

"Gorrie? What are you doing here? And just where is here?" Gideon was disoriented, not sure where he was.

"You're in the hospital, Gideon. Do you remember anything?" Gorrie was worried about his younger brother. None of them had ever been assaulted before and he had no idea what to ask or how to feel.

"I am? I think I talked with someone about what happened." Gideon reached to raise the head of the bed.

"You did. James was around but I don't know that you were alert enough to think clearly." Gorrie pulled his chair over and sat before he yawned. He glanced down at his watch. He was due in at work in a couple of hours and didn't know how he would make it through the day. Gorrie reached for his phone and sent a text off to another one of their brothers, Galway, and asked if he could help with Gideon that day. A quick positive response came through. Galway would be there shortly.

"What happened, Gorrie?" Gideon watched his brother, seeing the struggle that Gorrie was going through.

'You were assaulted in the church last night, Gid. You stepped in to protect Garnet Graeme. She was unhurt basically but you took the brunt of the assault." Gorrie watched his brother closely, seeing how hard Gideon was taking the fact that a young lady of his acquaintance had been in danger.

"I want to see her." Gideon pushed at the blankets, pausing as Gorrie shook his head

"It's early morning, Gid. You need to wait for at least a couple of hours." Gorrie looked around, feeling someone watching them. Only there was no one there. "What can you tell me?"

"I don't remember much, unfortunately. In fact, I only have flashes of someone attacking me. Garnet's okay?" Gideon didn't look at his brother, not wanting him to see the raw emotions that he knew were in his eyes.

"She apparently has some bruising on her wrist from what I was told. It's the psychological damage that we need to watch out for. And yes, I said "we". You're not on your own in this. Gemma is planning on approaching her at some point today. She knows her better than any of us, except maybe for you."

Gideon nodded, a hand on his jaw. He slept, not answering Gorrie's question. Gorrie watched for a moment before he too slept. Neither man saw the dark figure that appeared in the room and glared at Gideon before that man walked away. The nurses stared at the man before calling for security.

Garnet stared at her door later that morning. She had been hard at work as she worked through some copyrighting issues that she was having and had had to wait to answer the door. She peeked out, seeing Gideon standing there, his brother, Galway, and his sister, Gemma, there. Garnet leaned her head against the wall of the hall before she reached for the lock.

"Gideon?" Garnet's quiet voice had Gideon jumping. She frowned at him.

"Garnet? May we come in?" Gideon waited patiently for Garnet to respond. Galway was staring around, his back to the couple. Ginny moved past Gideon to hug Garnet.

Garnet finally nodded and stepped back to let them in. Her eyes were on Galway who simply stared back at her. She sighed. Someone was out there, she could tell. Her feeling that someone was watching her and following her had just been confirmed.

"Garnet? Are you okay?" Gideon's words were muffled to some degree. His jaw was too sore for him to speak correctly. He studied the lady in front of him, a crack appearing in his heart. Gideon had vowed never to marry, just why he could not say. Garnet had started working on his heart without him even being aware of that.

Galway had turned back to search the area once more and then turned back to the door. His eyes dropped to a package sitting on a wicker chair and reached for it. He frowned at it for a moment before he shrugged and headed into the house. He toed off his sneakers and then headed for where he could hear voices. He stopped just outside of the kitchen, watching the scene inside, a slight smile on his face. Gideon has met his match, Galway decided, watching the couple inside, seeing that Ginny was barely keeping her smile hidden.

Garnet stood across the wooden table from Gideon, hands planted on her hips. She was frowning at him. Gideon was staring back at her, a slight look of amusement on his face.

"Garnet? Are you okay?" Gideon finally spoke, concern evident in his voice.

Garnet shook her head, her arms wrapped around her abdomen. She wasn't sure how she felt. Not any more. The assault the night before had terrified her and shaken her to her core. She trusted that God would protect her. Garnet didn't know how He would do that.

"I don't know." She shifted on her feet, not taking her eyes from him. "And how are you?"

Gideon shrugged. His head was pounding with a vicious headache and his jaw was aching. He reached for a chair, sinking into it, not able to stand any more. He felt Galway's hand on his shoulder before his brother moved past him.

"Garnet? It's almost lunchtime." Ginny reached to hug the other lady, knowing that somehow their lives were now entwined in a way that they had not thought possible yesterday.

"It is?" Garnet blinked and looked around. "I have soup. If that works?"

"Anything is fine, Garnet." Ginny moved to the fridge. "May I?"

Garnet nodded, not sure what to do. Galway's hands on her shoulders shifted her to sit on a chair beside Gideon. He then nodded at Gideon before he moved to help Ginny to prepare their lunch.

Gideon's head tilted as he studied Garnet. His hand reached for hers, startling her for a moment. He continued to study the beautiful lady sitting beside him, hearing the quiet movement around him from Galway and Ginny.

Her eyes on Gideon, Garnet's mouth opened and closed. She was unable to say anything. Tears sparkled in her eyes for a moment before she drew in a deep breath. She had no words to say. Her eyes raised to the ceiling as she prayed for peace and protection.

Chapter 4

Garnet rose at last, helping to clear away the debris from their meal. She had watched Gideon as he had struggled to eat his soup, knowing that he had been hurt because of her. She didn't know what to say or how to help him.

Galway reached for the package, setting it on the table. He frowned at Gideon as his brother stared at him and then the box.

"Where did this come from, Galway?" Gideon's finger reached to touch him.

"It was on the porch. It's addressed to Garnet." Galway's attention turned to Garnet.

"It was?" Garnet stood at the table, staring down at it. "I wasn't expecting any packages. I have no one who would be sending me anything." She turned to reach for a sharp knife, slicing through the tape that sealed the package. Garnet drew in a deep breath. This was not what she was expecting.

Her hands folded back the flaps even as she drew in another deep breath. She was afraid, she had to admit, that something was dangerous in the box. Garnet stared into it, a frown appearing on her face.

Gideon had been focused on her, his eyes intent. As she hesitated to reach into the box, he was on his feet, an arm around her to support her. He too stared into the box before he raised his head to stare at Galway.

“What’s in it?” Ginny was curious about her brother’s reaction.

“A teddy bear?” Garnet reached to pull it out, feeling it all over. She frowned even deeper as she felt a hard lump in one of the stuffed bear’s legs and reached for the knife. She sliced through the fabric and reached into the slit, her slim fingers shoving aside the stuffing as she found the lump.

Gideon reached to take the item from her as she stared down at it.

“A thumb drive? What is this all about?” Gideon was not sure what to think. All he could do was pray for his lady despite the pounding heading and soreness of his jaw.

“We need to look at it.” Garnet moved away from them and then returned from her office with her laptop. “I can scan it to see if there is anything sinister on it.” She worked away, finding reaching to open the thumb drive. She stared at the material that was on it. “I don’t understand this. It’s not making any sense.”

The other three gathered around her, watching as she scrolled through the material that was on the screen. They read through it as she moved slowly through it all.

“Do you know these people, Garnet?” Gideon’s hands rested on her shoulders, bringing comfort to her that she didn’t understand.

“No, I can’t say that I do. I’m not from this town. In fact, I’m from Alberta, not Ontario. These people are from here." Garnet shifted to stare at the other three. "Do you know them?"

Galway nodded. He knew the people. He just didn't understand why Garnet would have received this information. He crouched down beside her chair, reaching to scroll back through the information.

"Can we print this, Garnet?"

Garnet nodded, reaching to print of numerous copies. On her feet, she headed for her office, pausing for a moment before she shook her head. There was no way that she knew these people. It was a mystery as to why she received this.

Gideon turned as he heard a tap on the door, heading that way. James stared at him before he shook his head.

"I should have known." James stepped inside, toeing off his shoes. "Where is Garnet?"

"In the kitchen. So are Galway and Ginny. We just opened a package that is bizarre and that none of us understand." Gideon walked back into the kitchen, taking the papers that Garnet was waving at him.

"Garnet? What did you go and do?" James gave her a quick smile before he stood and stared down at the tabletop. "What is all this?"

"I have no idea. Galway found the package on the front porch. It had this bear in it. This bear then had a thumb drive in it." Garnet pointed at the paperwork that he held. "This is what was on the thumb drive. I don't know these people."

James watched Garnet closely, seeing the stress and distress that she was trying hard to hide. His attention turned to the papers. As he reads through them, he frowned deeper. This was truly bizarre, he decided. He then began to pray for his friends. Once more, someone he knew was being targeted by someone.

Late that evening, Garnet curled up on the couch. She needed to retire but her mind was just too active to do that. She knew that she would not sleep. Garnet was puzzled still about what she had received. James had taken the box and the bear and asked to borrow the thumb drive for a few days. She had simply nodded her agreement to that.

Pulling a blanket over herself, Garnet reached for her Bible. She needed to find the promises of protection and peace and safety that were sprinkled throughout the Book. A notepad in her hand, Garnet made her notes before she set aside the notepad, pen, and her Bible. Her thoughts then turned to prayer, begging God for understanding, before she grew silent and just waited for God to speak to her. Her eyes closed and she slept, finding the peace that only God could provide to her.

Gideon sat on his back deck, his toe keeping the glider in motion. His head was back as he stared up at the stars, watching the moon as it moved slowly through the dark sky. He too was praying for peace but his prayers also included Garnet. She fascinated him, he decided, and he wanted to learn more about her.

James stared at the paperwork sitting on his desk. He was at home and should be retiring as well. He couldn't until he could understand what the paperwork was about. Only, there was no answer. James knew the names that were listed. He didn't understand the connection between Garnet and them. He sighed. He reached for his email and sent off an email to a friend with a copy of the paperwork, just asking her to do her best. And James knew that he would hear back by tomorrow with a brief outline of what she had found.

Chapter 5

Standing in his office the following Sunday morning, Gideon felt at his jaw. It was still very sore and bruised. He wasn't sure how he would manage to speak long enough to give his message. He turned as he heard a tap at the door and the board chairman stood there. Paul Rogers nodded to himself. He knew to a certain extent how Gideon thought.

"Gideon? You're not going to be able to speak that well this morning." Paul grinned at him.

"No, I don't know that I can. I'll do my best." Gideon was frustrated but also very worried about Garnet.

"That's okay. For today, we'll do one of our praise and prayer days. We haven't done it in a while. Give a brief message. Talk for as long as you can." Paul's hand was on Gideon's shoulder as he prayed for his friend and pastor.

"Thank you, Paul. That works. You're right. We do need to do this. I'm just worried that violence came into the church."

"Not your fault, Gideon. It's not your fault." Paul watched as Gideon paced. "How is Garnet?"

"Garnet? I'm not sure. I haven't spoken with her today. It's just so strange, Paul. Why go after her?" Gideon spun to stare at the older man. "She received a package which is also strange. She has a list of names as well, people who she doesn't know."

"She did? I gather that has been turned over to the authorities?" At Gideon's nod, Paul hesitated. "Would she share that with me? I may be able to help."

"We can ask her. She's coming to lunch with my family today. I didn't know that she had no one in town. And that she has no one at all from what she has said." Gideon was saddened at that.

"She doesn't? She has kept very quiet about that. Talk to her and have her call me tomorrow at the office." Paul was a lawyer and knew that Garnet may well need his assistance.

"I'll do that."

Garnet shifted restlessly in her pew. She had chosen to sit at the back of the sanctuary, ready to rise and run if she had to. Ginny had sat beside her, watching her new friend closely. She had spoken with Gideon about her. Only Gideon had not been very forthcoming about Garnet. Ginny could understand that but it didn't help her to help Garnet.

Walking away from everyone after church, Garnet hesitated before her phone was out. She simply sent a text message to Gideon, begging him to forgive her, but she just could not do the lunch with his family. Her phone was tucked away as she slid into her vehicle, not seeing Gideon's family watching her.

"She's hurting, isn't she?" Gorrie watched her closely, a frown on his face. He knew that Gideon was hurting for his lady but he would never say that to his brother.

"She is. This is when she needs family around her and from what little that she said, she doesn't have that. That has to hurt big time." Galway was frustrated as well, knowing that Garnet could well disappear and no one would find her. And that his brother would head out looking for her if that happened and likely end up hurt once more.

"Let it lie, Galway." Ginny wrapped an arm around her brother's. "I'll call her later to see if she needs anything. For now, we can pray for her. I'm sure that Gideon will find her eventually today."

Gideon stared at the text message, dismayed and a little hurt, he had to admit, that Garnet would not be at lunch with them. He stared into the distance before he sent a text to Gorrie and then drove off. He needed to find somewhere he could pray and that would be the beautiful garden in the centre of town. Gideon always felt closer to his God in that place, remembering how he had been prayed for in the garden so many years ago.

Rising from the bench that he had found hours later, Gideon stretched. He didn't see the man watching him who also rose and followed him. He was heading for his home and a late meal but first he sent Garnet a text message just to put his mind at peace that she was okay.

Garnet stared at the text message. She wasn't used to people asking if she was all right. That didn't happen in her world. It never had. She sighed. Gideon was just walking into her life and yes, she had to admit, into her heart. Garnet had observed him from afar over the months that she had been in Oak City. She saw the compassion and caring that he handed out to anyone and everyone. He went above and beyond when he needed to even if it exhausted him. She could appreciate that only too well. Her brother had been like that, particularly with his family. That had cost him his life when he tried to rescue their parents from a boating accident. All three had lost their lives ten years ago. Haunted by that, Garnet had fled her hometown and moved gradually across the country. It hadn't helped to dispel the memories or the sorrow. That she had wanted but never had been able to find no matter how much she had prayed for that.

Turning from her office, Garnet walked back through the house that she had rented. She was afraid, she had to admit, not sure why but she prayed for that fear to be removed. She sighed once more. Garnet fully understood that God sometimes allowed circumstances that would draw a person closer to Him. She felt sure that this was her time to do that. She just didn't want Gideon involved any more than he had been.

James turned from his front door after closing it quietly. He was exhausted. Being on call for the weekend had done that. There had been a number of investigations that he had been called out on and that worried him but puzzled him as well. There just seemed to be too many. James felt that somehow they were all related but he had no proof of that. He would need to speak with his supervisor, Lyle, and also the police chief, Toryn, when he was next in the office. James paused for a moment before he shook his head. He would follow up with Gideon the next day, a

Monday, knowing that Gideon took Mondays as an off day.

Gideon rose at last from the glider on his back deck. It was after midnight. He had spent hours in prayer, he was well aware, but that was not unusual for him. He stretched, his muscles stiff from his inactivity but he felt peace in his heart. He had learned early in life that prayer worked best in every situation. His parents had taught their seven children that as toddlers. His parents had been prayer warriors and he strived to be that as well.

He looked around as he heard a faint sound and then smiled as he saw a cat approaching. The calico cat from next door had come to find him. He reached to pick her up, cuddling her close. Her pink tongue came out to lick at his face before she settled into his arms. He turned and walked into his house, knowing that the cat would just stay for a while and then disappear through the door he had created in a wall beside the back door and head for home.

Chapter 6

Later that week, Garnet walked into a book store in town. She was bored, she decided. Her work as a copywriter no longer held her interest. In fact, she was actively looking for another position. She just wasn't sure that she should be at this point in time. Garnet wasn't sure at all that she should stay in Oak City no matter how well she liked the town and the people.

James had approached her the day before, asking if she had remembered who the man was. She had stared at him before shaking her head.

"I have no idea, James. I didn't recognize him. And as far as I know, I don't have any enemies. Have you identified him yet?" Garnet challenged him back, a smirk on her face.

James grinned at her. This was what he was beginning to understand how she thought.

"No, I haven't. I was hoping that you knew him and we could end it today." He grinned at her again for a moment before he sobered. "Gideon doesn't know either. He's still not sure what all happened that night. That's understandable."

"It is. I worry for him, James." Garnet leaned against her kitchen counter, folding her arms around herself. "He's vulnerable, James. How do we keep him safe?"

"We can't, Garnet, as much as we would like to. It's hard to do that. He is at the church and then out and about every day. Even when he's off, he's not at home a lot." James was frustrated at that.

"I get that, James. There has to be some way to do that."

"Well, there is one way." James tried to hide his grin but his eyes sparkled with mirth.

"And that would be?" Garnet glared at him, trying hard to hide her own smile.

"You two could date. That way you could keep track of Gideon and he could keep track of you." James waved as he walked away, hearing Garnet's protest behind him. He shut the front door behind him and leaned back on it for a moment. His thoughts were troubled. Unfortunately, without any new information, he had had to set the investigation to one side. It's not what James wanted to do.

Garnet moved to lock the door behind James, a hand resting on the lock for a moment. She was torn, she decided, not sure which way to turn. James' suggestion had not really surprised her. Gideon had called her every day, just to talk. She appreciated that but she worried about him.

Gideon walked towards Garnet. He had been visiting a church member at their place of employment and caught a glimpse of Garnet as she entered the book store. He searched for her, finding her standing and staring at a shelf of books, her hands deep in her pockets.

"Garnet?"

Gideon's voice beside her had Garnet jumping. She stared at him, her eyes huge with fright before she glared at him. His smile caused her to glare even more.

"Gideon? Are you supposed to be at the church or something?" Garnet's voice held traces of the fear that she had just felt.

"No. I was visiting a church member down here and saw you entering this store. I love this store." Gideon's eyes closed for a moment as memories surged through his mind. His eyes popped open. "Do you have time for a coffee?" He glanced at his watch. "Actually, it's lunchtime. Join me for a meal, Garnet?" He waited patiently for Garnet to respond, seeing the conflict that she was going through.

"I guess. I'm not working today. I took the day off." Garnet moved away from the store, Gideon keeping step with her. "Where are we eating?"

"We could go to the diner but I know of a nice little tea room just around the corner."

"A tea room? That sounds nice." Garnet entered the tea room and then hesitated, not sure where to sit.

"Over here. It's a favourite seat of mine." Garnet pointed to a table for two in a corner. He seated Garnet and then found his own seat. "May goes to our church. I'm not sure if you have ever met her."

Garnet shook her head. She didn't think that she had but she would make a point of searching for her on Sunday. She looked around, seeing the tea room was reaching its capacity and was grateful that Gideon had managed to find a table for them. Garnet reached for the menu, perused it and then looked up at Gideon, finding him staring at her.

Gideon stared at Garnet, taking in her beauty and just grateful that she had agreed to a meal with him. He had never been one to date or even ask a lady other than his family out for a meal. And here he was, sitting in a tea room and across the table to a lady. He decided right then that he didn't want to lose Garnet ever. He didn't realize that his heart was already taken by her.

"What would you like, Garnet?" He grinned at her as she frowned at him and then down at the menu.

"I have no idea. It all sounds so delicious."

"How be I order for us today? Next time, you can order." Gideon's grin widened as he saw May approaching them.

Garnet shrugged, not knowing what to say. She looked up as a hand was laid on her shoulder.

"Gideon? Who is this?" May smiled at Garnet.

"This is Garnet Graeme. You have likely seen her around the church."

"I have. I have wanted to speak with you, Garnet, but you're gone so quickly after the services." May moved to take the menus from in front of them. "What can we get you?"

"You know what I like. Can we do that for two?" Gideon waited for Garnet to agree, seeing her finally nod.

May watched the two carefully, a wonder on her face that Gideon was here with a lady. She prayed for her pastor and his lady as it seemed that Garnet was. She was well aware that he had been beaten protecting her. She sighed as she walked away. Another young friend in danger and all because of his lady.

Chapter 7

Later that night, Garnet stared at the letter she had found in her mailbox. She had not opened it. It was addressed to her with only her first name. She did not recognize the handwriting and that scared her. Garnet walked away from it, praying for protection and peace. She just didn't know if she would ever feel safe. She thought back and realized that she had not felt safe since her family had died.

Reaching for her phone, Garnet scrolled through her messages. A soft smile lit her face as she read Gideon's message simply thanking her for sharing a meal with him. She could see his smile as they had parted company with him promising that they would share another meal at May's.

Finally seeking her rest, Garnet was not able to settle down. She was jumping at every noise. And the letter that she had not opened was still on the kitchen counter. She was hiding from it, she knew, but also knew that she wanted James to open it, not her.

James stared at the letter the next morning, a frown on his face. He snapped on latex gloves and slit the envelope with his pocket knife. Pulling out the folded sheets of paper, James looked at Garnet. She was waiting for him to tell her what was in the letter.

"You don't recognize the handwriting?" James had to question her on that again.

"No, I don't. I have no idea who it is." Garnet tilted her chin towards the letter. "What does it say?"

"I have no idea. I haven't opened it yet." James unfolded the letter as he continued to stare at Garnet as he did so. He gave an inward sigh as his gaze dropped to the letter. He read it through before he read it through a second time. It made absolutely no sense.

Garnet was watching his face and then moved to stand beside him, reading the letter as he tilted it towards her.

"What are they talking about? I have nothing that isn't mine. I gave away or sold just about anything of my family's that I didn't want. I didn't keep a whole lot. My grief was too deep. Who is this?" Her finger stabbed at the paper. "I don't know this person."

"You don't?" James grew frustrated. This just added a wrinkle to the case that wasn't needed but had been expected. "Okay. I'll take this with me then. I'll let you take a photo of it, if you like."

"I do like." Garnet reached for her phone and snapped pictures of the letter. "Who is doing this, James? I don't know that I have any enemies. And Gideon is now involved, isn't he?" Garnet paced away from James and then spun to face him. "How do we keep him safe and away from me?"

James gave a quick grin. If he was reading Gideon correctly, he would not be kept away from Garnet. And if he was reading Garnet correctly, there was no way that she would stay away from Gideon. They made a couple that James had not seen coming but nodded that they suited each other.

“Okay, James. How do we do this? How do we find this person?” Garnet was deep in thought, trying to figure it all out.

“We don’t. I work on it.” James walked away, confident that Garnet would not keep away from the investigation. He was heading for Gideon but stopped his car and pulled to the side of the road. Gideon had a funeral that afternoon and he would not approach him yet.

Garnet paced her home before looking at her watch. She headed for her office, needing to log in and start her work as a copywriter. Her heart was not in it any more. She wanted to find Gideon and stay with him and that puzzled Garnet.

The two men watching Garnet’s home waited for her to exit the house but she never did. One left to find their employer and then headed for the church and the funeral. He tucked himself away in a seat at the back of the sanctuary. He stared at Gideon, keeping his emotions hidden and his face blank. He was under orders just to monitor what Gideon was doing and how much time he spent with Garnet. The man had no idea why he had been asked that but he had learned early not to ask any questions and to just do what he was ordered to.

Gideon’s heart was troubled. He concentrated on the service but his thoughts still slipped to Garnet, praying that she was okay. He wanted to be with her and protect her. Gideon just didn’t know what he was afraid of other than he was afraid that Garnet would walk away from him or be seriously hurt when he could not protect her.

That evening, Don, who had a security team, rang the doorbell to Gideon's home. He had been contacted by James who expressed concern about Gideon. Don had simply stated that he would find Gideon and speak with him.

Gideon frowned at Don before he gave a half-smile. He knew full well why Don was there. Don was a friend and had been through an adventure of his own.

"Don? I'm not surprised to see you. Who squealed?" Gideon's smile grew.

"James. He's worried about you, Gideon." Don toed off his shoes and headed for the kitchen. Their friendship was such that they felt comfortable helping themselves to coffee in one another's house. That had not changed when Don had married.

"I know he is. We just don't know why." Gideon headed back for the door, opening it to stare in surprise at Garnet. "Garnet? What are you doing here? Come. In with you." He reached to hug her, feeling her hugging him back.

Garnet stepped away, slightly embarrassed at hugging her pastor. She tilted her head as she heard water running in the kitchen.

"I'm sorry. I'll leave. You have company." She turned back to the door.

"It's okay, Garnet. It's Don. He's here to see what he can do to help us stay safe. He would have met with you separately but now that you're here, it's better. He can talk to us together." He stared down at her down-turned head. “I want to make sure that you stay safe.”

“I know that you do, Gideon. I want the same for you.” Garnet didn’t know how to express her thoughts or how much she was praying for just that.

“I know, love. I know.” Gideon didn’t realize that an endearment had slipped out. He didn’t see Don standing in the kitchen doorway watching them.

Don nodded to himself. They were a couple, just as James had hinted at. It would be difficult to keep Gideon safe, he knew. Gideon was all over the town and countryside, just to be there for his congregation. He would not change, that much Don was aware of.

Garnet jumped as she heard a slight sound behind her and spun, her eyes huge as she stared at Don. She recognized him from seeing him around town.

“You’re here?” Her voice was high-pitched just from her fright. She winced at the sound.

Don gave a brief grin.

“I am, Garnet. I am. We need to talk and right now, this is the best place to do so. Come on into Gideon’s kitchen. We have coffee if you want that.”

“Thank you, I think.” Garnet groaned to herself. Had she really said that? She was rusty with her social skills, she realized. She felt Gideon’s hand brush her shoulder as he sat beside her, his eyes on Don.

Chapter 8

Don moved back into the kitchen and reached for a chair to sit opposite Garnet. He studied her, his face neutral as he did so. His eyes watched Gideon and how he was reacting to her and nodded to himself. James was correct. There was interest there from both of them but they were dancing around it, not willing to commit to anything. Gideon would move forward in dating Garnet, Don knew. It was how it had been for his security team and also for Toryn, Oak City police chief and a good friend of his.

Garnet stared back at Don, a frown on her face. She felt Gideon's arm around her shoulders and leaned into him. This was not what she had expected at all.

"Don? Do we know each other?" Garnet spoke at last, puzzlement on her face.

"We have never formally met, Garnet, but we have likely seen each other at church. Do you know Delanie from a ladies' Bible study group?" At her nod, he grinned. "She's my wife and yes, we had an adventure. But that is not why I'm here. James asked me to meet with each of you. I just wasn't expecting to see you two together."

"I shouldn't be here." Garnet's hands landed on the table as she moved to push her chair away. Gideon's arm was still around her shoulder and a slight pressure from it kept her in her place.

"You need to be, Garnet." Gideon's voice held a slight tone of worry. "It saves Don from repeating himself." Gideon grinned at his friend.

"It does. Now, tell me what has been going on?" Don's notepad was out as he made notes. "No other letters or packages? No phone calls or text messages?"

The couple shook their heads, looking at one another in puzzlement.

"We haven't, Don." Gideon rubbed at his cheek. "My phone number is out there, but I don't know that Garnet's is. We haven't updated the church director in a couple of years."

"No, we haven't. Garnet? How much would your number be out there?"

Garnet thought about that.

"Not much. I don't give it out readily. I will take numbers and block my number when I call. It's something that I have always done. And you know, I don't know why. I've done that since my family died." Garnet drew in a shuddering breath but didn't say anything else.

"I see. Okay, so that could be why, but expect it to happen, Gideon. You've talked to the board?"

"I have. We have a plan in place if we need it." Gideon had hated to do that but he had felt that he had no other choice.

"Good. I'll reach out to them as well. Now, about your personal time. We need to make some plans just in case."

"We do. I just don't want to." Garnet shoved away from the table, almost running from the room. She heard Gideon calling out to her but she didn't stop. Inside her car, she drove away, blinking away the tears that threatened to fall.

Gideon stood in his driveway, dismay on his face as he watched Garnet leave. It was not what he wanted but he knew that she had to. His head turned as Don approached him.

"Gideon? Is she heading for home?"

Gideon shrugged. He had no idea. If Don had not been there, he likely would have taken off and found her. With Don here? He couldn't. He needed to finish his conversation with Don, no matter how much it hurt and worried him that Garnet had left like that.

"I would think so, but I don't know for sure. I'll call her later. Now, what do you have to say?" Gideon's attention was still not totally on Don.

"We'll talk, Gideon. I just need some information on whether you'll be away at any conferences or anything like that over the next few weeks." Don waited patiently once more for Gideon to respond, a slight smile on his face that he made no attempt to hide.

Gideon's eyes narrowed as he glared at his friend before he shook his head and his own grin came out.

"You just had to do that, didn't you?" Gideon pointed at the house. "Let's go back inside and I can go over my agenda with you. You'll need to talk with

Garnet. And that may be a challenge for you. This is when it would help to have ladies on your team."

"I know. I can ask Daci to talk with her." Daci's was Don's sister and was often pulled in to help him.

"That would work. Now, this is what I have coming up. I do need to be at a pastor's conference for three days next week. It's local, in Riverville, and I know that Abe and his team would help." Gideon was referring to friends of theirs. Abe also had a security team and helped out whenever he was asked.

Don stood beside his truck an hour later, his hand resting on the door handle before he pulled it open and then drove away. He was heading for Garnet. He just didn't know if she would speak with him. Pausing outside her home, he noted that the lights were all off. He couldn't be sure that she was home or not. He sighed and then shrugged, planning on catching up with her on the next day.

Garnet stood, watching through a crack in the drapes. She was afraid. The letter that had been waiting for her when she reached home had been brutal. She had no idea who was after her and that scared her deeply. She would reach out to James tomorrow, she decided, before heading for her office and pulling up her work on the computer. Garnet worked away for hours before she rose and stretched, a hand rubbing at her lower back as she walked towards her kitchen. She squinted at the clock and sighed. She had just pulled another all-nighter for work and needed to sleep.

Instead of making herself coffee, Garnet headed for her bedroom and lay down on her bed. A blanket was pulled over herself before she slept. Her dreams were troubled. She didn't realize that she was weeping as she slept, her fear driving her dreams. She was deeply afraid for Gideon, not realizing how much he was taking over her thoughts and emotions and that he was just walking in on her heart.

Chapter 9

James stepped back from Garnet's door late that morning. He had repeatedly rung the doorbell with no answer. He frowned before he walked around the house and then peeked into the garage. Her car was in it. She was just not answering her door. James had to walk away at last, knowing that he had to be elsewhere but he would return and when he did, Garnet would speak with him.

Don approached her home late that afternoon, his keen eyes searching the area for anything or anyone that did not belong there. He could feel himself watched as he did so but couldn't see anyone who stood out. He turned back to the door to find Garnet watching him from where she stood on the front porch.

"Don? You're here?" Garnet turned back into the house. She had just woken and was hungry. She headed for the kitchen and the sandwich that she had made herself before Don had appeared. "I just woke up, so please excuse me while I eat."

"Go ahead, Garnet. Eat your meal. May I walk through your home and assess it from a security standpoint?" Don patiently waited for Garnet to study her sandwich before she gave a brief nod.

Don walked back towards the kitchen. There was no security system. That had to change. He had reached out to his team and Caleb and Mark would head towards them with what they needed.

"Don? What did you decide?" Garnet reached for her coffee mug, wrapping her hands around it.

"You have no security system, did you know that?" Don's voice was stern.

"I know. I haven't needed it. But you think that I do?" Garnet was not backing down from Don. She prayed daily for protection and had not felt the need to have a physical system in place.

"You do, Garnet." Don pulled out a chair and sat, his portfolio landing on the tabletop. "I have two of my team heading this way to set up the system. For your own safety, we need to do this, Garnet." His voice was stern.

"I see. Yes, I guess that I do." Garnet stared at her coffee mug, not sure what to say or what to expect. "How invasive will it be?"

"Not invasive, Garnet. We'll set up sensors on the windows and doors, install some cameras and motion-sensitive lights outside, particularly on your doors and on the garage. The garage will have sensors there as well." Don reached for a paper in his portfolio. "This is what I would suggest. It's up to you how far we go but for your safety, I would certainly recommend putting everything in place."

Garnet studied the paper that Don slid across the table, her thoughts troubled. She began to pray, realizing that God would protect her but He would also expect her to take the steps that Don suggested. She had always felt that she needed to take physical steps that were available. God used physical things and people to ensure that His people were safe and taken care of.

"I see, Don. Okay, I guess. This is a rental house, you know?" She frowned at him.

Don grinned at her. He had been well aware that it was a rental home. He also knew who the landlord was.

"It's okay. Our police chief, Toryn, is your landlord. He didn't have time to set up the security on the house as he usually does. You rented it and moved in and he had been meaning to speak with you. Life got in the way." Don nodded towards the paper. "He has agreed to do all this. And you are not paying for it. He is. It's what he does for his tenants."

"I see. Okay then. You're working on it now?" Garnet was on her feet, pacing around the table.

Don watched her pace before he pulled out his phone. Mark was outside with Caleb and were beginning their assessment.

"Two of my security team are here. They'll work away at what they need to do outside first and then move inside. What can I do for you in the meantime?" Don prayed for Gideon's lady, afraid suddenly for her.

"I have no idea." She glanced at her watch. "If you will excuse me, I do need to get to work." She walked away, leaving Don watching her as she did so before he headed outside to confer with the two men.

Garnet sat in front of her computer, her fingers on the keyboard. She was lost in thought before she shook her head and looked up. Her prayer was constant, a prayer for understanding, peace, and protection. She knew that Gideon had sent her a text message which she had not yet read. She would at some point.

Don walked through the house a few hours later, nodding to himself. Mark and Caleb had finished the system and headed for home. Don would soon as well. He paused in the office doorway, watching Garnet for a moment before she looked up at him.

"Garnet? Do you have a few moments so that I can go over everything with you?"

Garnet nodded and was on her feet to do a walk-through with Don. She sighed as she locked the door behind him, her eyes turning towards the kitchen. That letter still sat on the countertop and needed to be dealt with. She walked back towards her office, to finish off what she needed to before she headed for her bedroom. Stretching out on her bed, Garnet began to weep, her thoughts turning to prayer before she slept.

Gideon set his phone to one side. Garnet had not responded to his text message and that worried him. He sighed to himself before he too spent time in prayer, his list of people to be prayed over just continuing to grow.

The next morning, Garnet hesitantly entered the police department building and asked for James. The letter was clasped tightly in her hand. The desk officer eyed her keenly before reaching for the phone and calling for James.

James stood just out of sight of Garnet. He frowned that she had appeared here. He had planned to reach out to her later that day. Something had to have happened for her to have appeared here. He walked towards her, taking the visitor badge that he was handed.

"Garnet? You're worried about something?" James' questions had Garnet spinning around to face him.

"I am. I got this yesterday or the day before. I can't remember which. I haven't opened it. I can't." She thrust the letter towards him, almost dropping it from her trembling hands.

James caught it between his two hands, a frown appearing on his face. Garnet was afraid, he could tell, and that was not what he had expected.

"Come on to my office, Garnet. We'll take a look at it." James had a quiet word with the desk officer who nodded and then reached for the phone once more, this time to have a crime scene tech meet James in his office.

Chapter 10

James set the letter down before he reached a hand out to Garnet, forcing her into a chair. He reached for a bottle of water and folded her hand around it. That she was deeply distraught was obvious.

The tech worked quickly with the letter, opening the envelope and then sealing the envelope and the letter into separate evidence bags. He nodded at James before he gathered up what he had been working with and departed for the lab.

James prayed for the lady in front of him. Once more, he was well aware that God was in control and that He only wanted the best for those who were His children. Unfortunately, James had seen too much and knew that God's best could involve life and death struggles.

"James? What did the letter say?" Garnet's hesitant question broke into his thoughts.

"The letter? It is very vague, Garnet. Merely states that you will do what you're asked to or that you will face the consequences. Any idea of what that means?" James kept his face neutral as he stared down at the letter. "It doesn't say what they want you to do or what the consequences are."

"They'll be following me, won't they? They'll go after anyone who I am around. I guess it's good that I don't have friends here." Garnet drew in a deep quivering breath, sorrow on her face at that thought.

"You do have friends, Garnet. Our friends want to be your friends. I'm your friend as is Gideon. We have a large group of friends who want to meet you. I understand that Don and Delanie are planning a meal on Saturday which includes you."

"Don mentioned something last night. Did you know that your police chief owns the house that I rent?" She scowled at him as he began to laugh.

"I do, Garnet. And I understand that Don and his team have been around to make it safer for you."

"They have. I just don't know what to think about all this. I have no enemies that I know of. I work as an independent copywriter. There is just not one employee. I take assignments through my website and then go on from there. I don't think that I have any enemies through that." Garnet spent some time mulling over her contacts before shaking her head. "I'm sorry, James. I just don't know what to say or think."

James nodded. It was not the first time he had heard something like that and it would not be the last time. He would likely have to set aside the investigation as there was just not enough evidence to continue it. And that felt so wrong, he decided.

Garnet walked away from the police department after a while. James and she had come to no conclusion on what the letter meant. She was frustrated at that. She paused for a moment, her eyes searching the area. Someone was out there and not someone who was on her side.

Gideon approached Garnet, startling her. He reached for her hand, drawing her away from the area and to a park bench where he forced her to sit before he sat beside her.

"Garnet? What happened? And don't tell me that nothing did." Gideon's voice was stern yet compassionate.

"I received a letter, Gideon, that just told me to do what I was asked to or face consequences. I have no idea who it was." Garnet drew in another quivering breath.

"I see. And you saw James?" At her nod, he looked at their clasped hands. "What can I say or do to help?"

"I have no idea, Gideon. I don't want you hurt and I know that will happen again if we let it."

"I'm not staying away from you. Understand that, Garnet. You're important to me." Gideon didn't say that he had already fallen in love with her and had acknowledged that to himself in the early morning hours. He didn't think that she was ready for that.

"It hurts, Gideon. I don't know why and I want to. I don't understand any of this." Garnet looked up at him.

"We don't have enough information to understand anything, Garnet. Listen. Our friends are planning a potluck dinner on Saturday. Will you go with me?" Gideon bit at his lip as he saw the surprised look on her face. This was the first time that he had ever asked a lady out for a meal.

Garnet stared at him for a moment. Then, she stared at the sky, praying through what her answer would be. She didn't want to hurt Gideon but she had real reservations about dating a minister and a popular one at that. Garnet looked back at Gideon, seeing that if she refused, he would be okay with that.

"I guess. James mentioned that Don and is it Delanie were planning something."

"It is Delanie and yes they are. We're meeting at Don's place. He has a lot more room than any of the rest of us." He rose, tugging her to her feet as well. "You need to get home, don't you?"

Garnet nodded, her hand nestling tighter into Gideon's. She felt cherished and loved and very important to someone, something that she had prayed for over many years. Garnet began to praise God in her heart, knowing that He had brought Gideon into her life at that point and that He would lead them as they walked through this adventure.

Gideon tucked Garnet into her car and then followed her home. He walked her to her door, unlocked it, gave her a hug, and then walked away. He had visitations that he needed to be about but he just wanted to stay with Garnet.

Garnet roused during the night, something feeling off. She was on her feet, creeping from window to window, drawing the drapes aside just enough so that she could look out. From the living room window, she watched the two men who crept away from her home. Something had happened out there. Garnet drew back from the window, a hand to her throat. She was terrified, she had to admit.

Wrapping herself in a blanket, she curled up on the couch, not wanting to sleep but her body had other ideas. She slept, awakening in the morning. She frowned at her watch. It was late and she needed to be up and about but she had no wish to do just that.

Chapter 11

Gideon hit his hands and knees, his head hanging down from the shock of being slammed into from behind. He was gasping for breath before an arm wrapped around his abdomen. He sat back on his heels, his head hanging down as he tried to draw in a deep breath and was unable to. Gideon had approached the church Saturday morning, intending to go back over his message for the next day and then spend time in prayer for the members of his congregation. He always prayed for each member of the church, begging God to speak to each one through his message. He always felt that it was God speaking through him, not him speaking his own words.

Another blow caught him on the back of the head, sending him to the floor of his office where he lay still, trying to recover his breath. His vision had darkened as he hit the floor. He didn't hear the men leave or feel the letter dropped to his back.

Thomas, one of Don's men, hesitated at the church door. It was unlocked, which Gideon had said it would be but he had not heard any movement from Gideon. If Gideon heard the church door, he was always there to greet whomever it was. This time, he wasn't. Thomas glanced at his watch. It was only mid-morning and Gideon had told him to drop in.

Searching through the church, Thomas' fingertips touched Gideon's office door. The door swung open slowly under his touch. It was dull inside before he reached for the light switch. He blinked for a moment as he adjusted to the light. Looking around, his mouth opened to call for Gideon before his eyes dropped. A cry was wrenched from him before he was on his knees, turning Gideon over and then checking for vital signs.

Gideon stirred as he heard Thomas' voice. He struggled to sit upright, Thomas' arm bracing him.

"Thomas? You're here?" Gideon was disoriented for the moment as his head started to clear.

"Gideon? What happened? I found you out cold and on the floor." Thomas reached for the letter. "And what is this?"

"What? A letter? I have no idea." Gideon was on his feet, shaking off Thomas' hands. "I'm okay, Thomas. Just had the breath knocked out of me. What is this letter?" Gideon reached for it, his fingers reaching for the unsealed flap before he pulled out the letter.

Thomas had no qualms about moving to read it over Gideon's shoulder. They frowned at each other. It was nothing but garble, a bunch of words strung together that made no sense. Gideon shrugged before he tucked it back into the envelope and then the envelope into his pocket.

"You need to be assessed at the hospital, Gideon." Thomas tried to draw him from the office.

"No. I'm fine. I've been hurt worse playing sports." Gideon squinted at Thomas. "You were to come here for a reason."

"I was. I wanted to go over the security system here. It's that time of year that we always do that." Thomas walked away, his thoughts and prayers with his pastor. Gideon would just refuse help, that much Thomas knew.

Gideon sighed as he reached for his office chair and sat, his eyes on the letter. He shook his head. It was not his priority right now. Instead, Gideon reached for his sermon for the next day, his head bowing as he began to pray over it.

Thomas approached the office a couple of hours later, tapping at Gideon's office door. He watched as Gideon looked up and then waved him in.

"All done, Thomas?" Gideon leaned back in his black leather desk chair.

"I am. We need to go back over your house as well and tighten up your security. We can do that next week." Thomas glanced down at his watch. "Are you about done?"

"I am." Gideon had tidied away his notes into a folder and set it to one side. He frowned at Thomas for a moment.

"Let me pray with you, Gideon, and then we'll head out. Take that letter with you." Thomas pointed at the envelope on the desk. "James will want to see it."

"I know that he will. I just don't know that there's anything in it." Gideon tucked the letter into a pocket. "Let's pray then, Thomas, and be on our way."

He glanced at the wall clock. "I'm due to pick up Garnet in about an hour."

Thomas' hand paused as he was rubbing it on his jeans leg.

"You're dating?" At Gideon's nod, Thomas studied his friend. "I'm glad. Garnet needs someone in her life and so do you."

Garnet was pacing her hallway. Gideon was due shortly but she felt unsettled and uncertain as to whether she should be going to this potluck dinner. She had been given a list of names for everyone who might be there and she recognized the names from church. Garnet had studied the younger couples in church over the year that she had been there. She had been envious of the ladies, seeing how the men in their lives treated them. It was how her father had treated her mother. She wanted that for herself. Now that Gideon had stepped in, she was uncertain if she was doing the right thing.

Gideon studied Garnet as she locked the door behind herself and then turned to face him. He reached to hug her, finding her standing still for a moment before she hugged him back. A prayer was whispered in her ear. He then reached for the bag that she had in her hand.

"Okay, love?" Gideon reached for her hand and led her to his car, tucking her inside and placing the bag on the floor in the back seat.

"I am, I think." Garnet's voice was quiet. "I'm just not sure about today."

"I know you are. So am I. We could be bringing danger to our friends. Toryn will be there as will James. Besides that, Don's security team is there. We should have enough people around to protect us." Gideon bit at his lip before he reached for her hand. "Garnet? Are you sure you're okay?"

Garnet stared down at their hands. She could feel the strength of his character in his grasp.

"I think so, Gideon." She looked up at him, a puzzled look on her face. "Just what are you saying?"

"That you are a beautiful lady. I love you, Garnet. It may be too soon to tell you that, but I do love you." He reached to kiss her cheek. "We'll talk, love. As to right now, we're due at a dinner. And there's this." He handed over the envelope. "I was assaulted this morning and that was left."

"Gideon!" Garnet was shocked and then she realized that she wasn't so shocked after all. She opened the letter, frowning at it. "This is just gibberish. Or is it?" She concentrated on the letter, not following the path that Gideon was driving.

"You're not sure that it's gibberish?" Gideon pulled to a stop near the cars parked at Don's. "What do you mean?"

"I think that it's in code of some kind. I need to work on it." She didn't move. Instead, her lips were moving as she read the words.

"Leave it for later, love." Gideon gently took the letter from her, placed it back into the envelope, and tucked it away before he came around the car and took her hand to help her out of it. He didn't let go of her hand as they walked towards the back of the house where their friends had gathered.

Chapter 12

The group turned as the couple arrived, calling out greetings or coming to hug them. Garnet felt overwhelmed for a moment before Don's sister, Daci, wrapped an arm around her and pulled her away from Gideon and towards the group of ladies. Gideon stood for a moment, a smile on his face, as he watched how the ladies' group just opened up to include his lady. He turned as he felt a hand on his shoulder.

Toryn stood there, a frown momentarily on his face. He didn't like that danger had come to Gideon, a man who seemed to have no enemies.

"Gideon, before we let it go for today, are you okay? You look a little rough."

"I am. I was assaulted this morning at the church. I didn't see the man but he left a letter for me. Garnet thinks that it's in code of some kind."

"She does, does she? Show me later." Toryn walked away, his frown easing as Don approached him.

"Toryn?" Don's gaze shifted to where Gideon was talking with some of his team members.

"We'll talk later, Don. Things are changing for Gideon and I don't like it." Toryn rubbed at his cheek.

"We will. Thomas was through the church this morning and tightened up the security there. He's planning on heading for Gideon's home on Monday."

"Thanks." Toryn was lost in thought for a moment. "This has never made sense. Gideon has no enemies that we know of but it is always possible that he does. We don't know enough about Garnet to know if she does or not."

Don was nodding. He had taken the opportunity to reach out to a friend and asked for her help. Emma had promised to research both Gideon and Garnet once she was back from her vacation.

Late that night, Gideon shifted on his glider. He had found his favourite seat. Staring up at the clouds that were scudding across the darkening sky, his thoughts were troubled for a moment. He began to pray through his thoughts as he always did and found the peace that God gave him. Gideon's head went back on the glider, his eyes closing for a moment. A smile crossed his face as he thought back over the day. Garnet had been welcomed completely by his friends' group. He could see how happy she had been by the smile that didn't seem to leave her face. Paul had approached him just before they left, a question on his face.

"Gideon? How serious are you about Garnet?" Paul had waited patiently for Gideon to think through his question.

"Serious enough, I think. I have told her that I love her. I just think that it was too soon." Gideon had hesitated to admit that.

"Not at all. You want to protect her as well, don't you?"

"I do. And I don't know how to do that." Gideon had looked stressed at that.

"God will protect you two. It may not be in the way that you expect. We all went through that." Paul looked around as a hand touched his arm and then swept that arm around his wife, Payton. "I would suggest that our ladies meet with Garnet. They can pray with her, share their stories with her, and then provide advice for her that comes from a woman's perspective. We can't do that."

Payton had been nodding at that.

"I have already approached her about that. She's going to come to our ladies' prayer and Bible study group. She admitted that she has no friends." Payton was saddened at that.

"No, she has said that." Gideon was puzzled at that. "I guess our group will help that out."

"As much as she will let us. And right now, she's not sure that she should." Toryn's wife, Slaney, had approached their group.

"No, she's not sure about that. I think all of our ladies were." Toryn stood with an arm around his wife. "And we can't force her."

Gideon nodded, his eyes on Garnet as she hesitated to approach them. His outstretched hand was quickly grasped by her and he pulled her close to him, not dropping her hand as she expected him to.

"Okay, love?" Gideon eyed her as she nodded. "We need to leave, Garnet, but I'm not sure that you're ready to."

“It’s okay, Gideon. We do need to leave. I’ve said my thanks.” Garnet waited for Gideon to do the same before they walked to his car. She had been surprised as he dropped a kiss on her cheek as they stood at her open front door and knew that he would wait until she had locked the door behind herself.

Gideon came back to the present, a frown crossing his face. Something was off, he decided, but he had no idea what. He knew that he was being followed. He had had glimpses of the men who were tracking him but they had not been close enough for him to get a clear enough description of them. He worried about his congregation and had spoken at length with the church board. They had all reassured him that they were not worried about that, that with the police officers who attended the services, they would work out a schedule for them to monitor the services.

He rose at last to seek his rest, his mind on the service the next day. He smiled as he thought about the day. Garnet had been overwhelmed at one point, he knew, just by the welcome that had been extended to her. He had been glad for that. He had fallen more in love with Garnet that day and he knew that it was likely obvious to his friends. He didn’t mind.

Pulling the covers over him at last, Gideon felt his body relaxing and he slept. He didn’t hear the slight movement outside of his home. He would not find out what had been left there for a couple of days and that discovery would force him to make a decision that he had not been prepared to make.

Chapter 13

Sunday found Gideon frowning down at the desk in his church office. An envelope lay on top of the folder that held his sermon. He hadn't placed it there. His office door had been locked when he arrived, just as he had left it the day before. Only his secretary held a key to the office and she had been away on holidays, not due back until Tuesday. This was puzzling.

Looking around as he heard a noise, Gideon beckoned Joshua, another one of Don's team members, into the office. He pointed to the envelope.

"What's wrong with that?" Joshua was puzzled. He leaned over to read the letter and saw Gideon's name on it.

"This. This letter. It wasn't here when I locked up yesterday." Gideon was growing angry and had to pray through that.

"It wasn't? Let me see your video feed." Joshua was in Gideon's desk chair and waiting as Gideon pulled up the application on the computer and then reached for the folder.

"Work away on that, Joshua. Catch up with me after the service." Gideon walked away to meet for pre-service prayer with the service team. He desperately wanted Garnet to be part of that group. He was ready to ask her to marry him at that point but he wasn't sure how she felt. She had not said as yet.

Garnet was seated in the back pew, Toryn and Slaney on one side of her, Daci on her other. She felt comfortable being there but she was still afraid. She didn't like that feeling. It had not been part of her life ever. Not knowing who it was or why was what was driving Garnet's fear. She listened carefully to Gideon's message of peace and security and hope. She found the fear disappearing to some extent.

Slaney watched Garnet carefully over the morning. Her hand had reached to clasp Garnet's lightly at one point, causing Garnet to jump and then smile at her. Slaney and Toryn had talked long the night before and Slaney had been determined to reach out to Garnet and make her one of her close friends.

Gideon walked to where Garnet was standing in the church entry. He was the last one to leave. Joshua had caught up to him and he hadn't liked that someone from the church had a key to his office other than himself and his secretary. That wasn't what they were to have. He would need to call in a locksmith and change the locks tomorrow. The letter had been handed over to James unopened. James had stared at it as he listened to Joshua tell him who had left it, his face paling slightly and then growing stern. Gideon had walked away before James could say anything.

A smile on his face, Gideon reached to hug Garnet before he took her hand and walked from the church with her, the church security system set and the door locked behind him. He had asked Garnet to spend the day with him. She had readily agreed.

"Where are we eating lunch?" Garnet smirked at him.

"How be we pick up something and find a spot by the river?" Gideon headed for a local sandwich shop that he frequented.

"Sounds like a plan." Garnet watched as he ran into the store and then back to his car. "Thank you, Garnet."

"For what?" Garnet was puzzled.

"For spending today with me. For being who you are. For bringing joy to my life. I meant it when I said that I love you. I am putting no pressure on you with that statement. If you can't or don't love me, I'll live with that." Gideon drove away, heading for his favourite spot on the river bank.

Three hours later, Garnet sat back on her hands, flushed with laughter. Gideon had made it a point to cause her to laugh. He had grinned unrepentantly at her when she told him to stop.

"I have enjoyed this, Garnet. Thank you." He reached for her hand and kissed the back of it.

"I have too, Gideon." Garnet bit at her lip. "Gideon, you have a large family. What would they think about us dating?"

"They are fine with it, Garnet. I have heard from each of them, asking me why we aren't dating. We are a large family, noisy at times, but we love one another and have each other's backs when needed. In case you didn't catch on, they are pushing for us to date." Gideon grew sober. "But I only want to do that if you do."

Garnet nodded. He had spoken just as she had expected him to.

"I guess, Gideon. I'm just worried about who is after us. And which one of us are they after?" Garnet studied him. "What happened today?"

"There was a letter on my desk this morning. We know who left it. They had a key to the office that they should not have had." Gideon was frustrated at that. "I have to have the lock changed tomorrow."

"I see. And you want someone with you? I can be there. I took this week off."

"You did? What a coincidence! So did I." Gideon continued to grin as she shook a finger at him. "What can we do this week that is fun?"

"Fun? Okay. I think I can come up with something." Garnet bit at her lip as she looked across the river. "What you told me, Gideon? That you love me? I love you too. It's too soon, isn't it?"

"I don't think so. God can and will bring love to couples quickly." Gideon wrapped her in his arms, a kiss on her temple. "We'll take it as slow or as fast as you want."

"We're dangerous to one another, Gideon. If we become a couple, it gets worse, doesn't it?"

Gideon nodded before he sighed. Garnet was correct. They were dangerous to one another and it would get much worse, that much he knew from what his friends went through. If they could only get some sense of why, they would be able to find the people responsible.

Neither Gideon nor Garnet saw the two men who stood close to them, listening to their conversation. They would not be able to describe them, their thoughts not on their adventure but on one another. They walked back towards the parking lot, passing the two men who followed them. They had no idea of what was facing them. All they knew was that they loved one another and that God was guiding them on the path that they were walking.

Chapter 14

James fingered the evidence bag that held the letter and envelope Gideon had found on his desk. He was highly disturbed that it seemed to have been placed by a member of the church. That member should have had no access to Gideon's office. Gideon had called early on the Monday morning, wanting to know when James was going to open the letter.

"I've opened it already, Gideon. We need to talk. And I need to talk with Garnet as well." James' voice was stern. He was struggling to control his emotions this time.

"I can arrange that. Where do you want to meet?" Gideon reached for his keys, intending on heading for Garnet's home.

"Here. I'll be waiting for you." James set his phone aside before he reached once more for the evidence bag. He was puzzled, he had to admit, by the tone and words of the letter. It was not making sense. James frowned and then reached for the copy of the previous letter. He nodded. These two letters went together. James reached for a pen and began to scribble away before his phone ringing interrupted him. On his feet, he headed for his car, needing to be on a crime scene.

Gideon reached for Garnet's hand as he helped her from the car. He glanced around, pulling her towards a jewelry store. Garnet pulled back, a question on her face.

"Gideon? What are you up to?"

Gideon paused, hesitation in his bearing.

"I love you, Garnet. You love me. Will you marry me? I know that we don't know each other well but what we're going through will push us into that knowledge. I don't want you on your own. I want to be the one to love you through our lives and to be the one who protects you to the best of my ability and as God wills." He watched her, his heart on his face.

Garnet stared at him, hearing his words in her head but reading his heart in his eyes. She sighed. He just had to do that, didn't he? Ask her to marry him right there on the street when she felt vulnerable. She finally nodded, finding herself wrapped into a hard hug before her hand was in his again and he was leading her through the store door.

Gideon waved at the store owner, one of his prayer partners on the church board. Jason nodded to himself. This was not unexpected. He moved towards where the trays of engagement rings were sent in the display cabinets.

"Gideon? Garnet? What can I help you with today?" He smiled kindly at the young lady, seeing her hesitation and yet the underlying joy on her face.

"An engagement ring, Jason. Garnet has agreed to be the bride of my heart. We love one another." Gideon's smile was huge. He had forgotten for the moment the danger that was a gathering storm around them.

“She has, has she? Garnet?” Jason’s look turned to Garnet, who was nodding.

“We do love one another, Jason. It just seems too soon. And I worry about the danger that is around us.” Garnet bit at her lip for a moment. “God is not saying no to us going through this.”

“And He would if it was not His plan for you. Now, what ring would you like to see?” Jason waited for them to make their decision.

“A ruby, please, Jason.” Gideon had long thought about the kind of stone that he would want for his bride. Nothing but a ruby would do.

Garnet stared at him before her face softened. She knew what passage of the Bible that he was referring to.

James watched the couple walk towards him not that long afterwards. He frowned. Something different was about them and he had no idea what it would be but he was sure that at some point, they would tell him what it was.

“Gideon? Garnet? Do you have time to talk with me?” James grinned at the couple.

“We do, James. Where do you want to meet?” Gideon tugged Garnet with him as James turned back to the police department building.

Garnet stared at the copies of the letters, her mouth moving as she read the words.

“These go together. The first words on each page start off a sentence. We just don’t know how many pages are missing. Who is doing this?”

"I don't know, Garnet. I had thought that was how it seemed with the letters. We need you two to be as careful as you can." James watched them walk away, a frown on his face. Something had changed with them but he could not put his finger on it. He shrugged and knew that they would tell him eventually. He just prayed that it was not more bad news.

Garnet stared at the house that Gideon had stopped in front of.

"You should be working, shouldn't you?" Garnet looked everywhere but at him.

"No, it's my day off. This is Gorrie's home. He and Belle are home. They'll welcome you to the family. As the oldest in the family, he's taken our parents' place in things like this when they are away." Gideon wrapped Garnet into a hug before he bent his head and kissed her.

Garnet was surprised at his action but accepted it. She turned to face the house, finding Gorrie standing near them, a delighted smile on his face.

"Gideon? Have something to share?" Gorrie reached to hug his brother and then surprised Garnet by hugging her as well.

"We do. We're engaged, Gorrie. I know. I know. It's sudden but we love one another." Gideon wrapped Garnet into his arms, resting his chin on the top of her head.

"You are? Congratulations, you two. Come on in. Belle had a suspicion that something was up. You know how she is.” Gorrie headed for the house, calling for Belle.

“It’s okay, love. They’ll overwhelm you at first and then back off until you get used to them.”

“I get that and appreciate it. It’s just what we’re going through. I don’t want them to be hurt.” Garnet felt bereft for a moment, not having her own family there to share the happiness and moment with her.

“You’re missing your family.” Gideon prayed for her, his words bringing comfort to her heart.

Chapter 15

Gideon waited patiently for Garnet to make a move towards the house. She didn't. She couldn't, she decided. Instead, Garnet turned back towards his car. She was feeling very overwhelmed by what had happened and wanted to find solace somewhere. Gideon's arms wrapped around her to hold her against him.

"Love? What's wrong?" Gideon's voice was low, just loud enough for Garnet to hear him.

"I don't know, Gideon. I really don't know. Something is about to happen and we can't stop it." Garnet stared around wildly at the street, focusing on a car that was parked across the street. It was empty but still caused her to fear. "That car? Gideon? Do you recognize it?"

Gideon studied it before he shook his head. He was not familiar with the vehicles on Gorrie's street.

"No, I don't, Garnet. Is it bothering you?"

"It is. And I don't know why." Garnet spun in his arms, hugging him. "What is going on, Gideon?" Her eyes caught movement and then her scream split through the air.

Gideon tried to turn but a sudden shove from behind him sent him stumbling forward. His feet tangled with Garnet's and then they were tumbling to the ground. His shout brought Gorrie and Belle to the front porch. Gorrie's hands raised as a weapon was pointed at him. He could hear Belle's quiet voice behind him and knew that she was calling for assistance.

Garnet hit the ground hard, her head bouncing off of it. Her vision darkened for a moment before she felt Gideon's weight holding her down. She struggled to shove him away, hearing his voice telling her to stay still. Garnet finally stopped moving, her eyes on Gideon's face as he shifted from protecting her with his body to the ground beside her. His eyes were on the man holding a weapon on his brother and his wife. This was what Gideon had feared, that whoever it was after himself and Garnet would go after his family.

Gorrie locked eyes with Gideon, his face expressionless. He didn't want to do anything that would cause one of them to get hurt. The man didn't lower his weapon. The other two men stood close to Gideon and Garnet, deep in conversation. Their conversation was low enough that neither of the couples could hear what was being said.

Gideon's arm was across Garnet, holding her in place on the ground. She had shifted to her side to face him. Her eyes were on the men behind him, fear on her face. Garnet whimpered slightly. Gideon's eyes dropped to her for a moment before his arm tightened around her. She could hear his whispered prayer.

Gideon's eyes went back to his brother. He frowned Gorrie. He was also thankful that Gorrie and Belle's young teen children were not home at the time. They were away with another of Gideon's and Gorrie's siblings on a camping trip.

The two men behind Gideon had moved towards him until they were almost touching him. Their gaze flickered between Gideon and Garnet and Gorrie and Belle. Their concentration was such that they didn't hear the quiet footsteps behind them until their wrists were caught, their weapons shaken from their hand, and then their wrists were drawn behind them and handcuffs slapped around them.

Officers approached the man standing in front of Gorrie, repeating the movements. The three men were shoved away from the two couples. Gorrie wrapped Belle in his arms, his eyes closing in relief.

Gideon sat upright, pulling Garnet to him. He wrapped her tightly in his arms, feeling her arms around his neck. All he could do was praise God for protecting them.

Garnet finally struggled to free herself from Gideon's hold, sitting back on the ground to stare at the officers who moved around them. She was puzzled at what had happened.

"Gideon? What was that all about?"

"I have no idea, love. Here. Let's go find Gorrie and Belle." Gideon was on his feet, his hand reaching for Garnet's hand to pull her to her feet. They walked towards Gorrie only to be stopped as an officer stepped in front of them. He sighed. "We need to give statements, don't we?"

"You do, Gideon. Over here for now." The officer pointed behind them. "You two need to be over there and separate."

Garnet sighed. This is not what she had expected today. She was frustrated at that. It should have been a happy day and had been until now. She felt Gideon's hand holding hers as they walked to the driveway and then moved to stand apart from one another. Garnet was well aware that Gideon was not happy to have to stand where he was; yet they had no choice

James hesitated for a moment before he headed for Gideon. This was not what he had expected, he knew. His eyes found Garnet's as she stared at him and then turned her attention to Gideon. He knew that she was giving her statement but he still wanted to talk with her himself.

"Gideon? What happened?"

"I don't know exactly, James. I really don't know. We were walking towards Gorrie when we were taken to the ground. I don't understand. Do you?" Gideon kept his eyes on his lady. He didn't understand what had happened. It happened all too quickly.

Garnet spoke almost too quietly for the officer to hear her words. He sighed to himself. There was just not enough information for them to understand what had happened. He eyed the men before he nodded. They had been hanging around the downtown area for the last week or so.

James walked towards Garnet. His head tilted as he studied her. She's angry, he decided, and that could be either good or bad.

"Garnet? What are you thinking?" James waited patiently for Garnet to speak. He had learned that it would take her time to think through what she wanted to say and then respond.

"I don't know what to think, James. What do you suggest that I think?" Garnet brushed past James, her hand reaching for the one that Gideon had stretched out for her to take.

"Okay, love?" Gideon dropped a kiss on her temple as he walked her towards Gorrie and Belle. "We'll talk, love, and try to make sense of what happened."

Garnet snorted, causing Gideon to grin at her before he pulled her up the steps towards Gorrie and Belle.

"Gorrie? You two are okay?" Gideon was worried about his oldest brother.

"We are and so are you two. Come on in. We need to talk, Gideon, and talk a lot. But first, you were coming here for a reason, I think, other than to be threatened on our lawn." Gorrie studied his brother, sensing that something had changed for his brother.

"We do need to talk, Gorrie, and we will." Gideon stared down at the lady who had claimed his heart. "Let's get inside and away from all this. Belle? I know you. You'll have coffee and treats ready."

"I do." Belle reached to hug Gideon and then Garnet.

Chapter 16

James walked towards Lyle's office, not sure what to think. The three men were not talking but their identities had been confirmed. They were wanted in numerous jurisdictions for numerous charges including murder. He didn't think that this case would go forward very quickly against them.

Lyle looked around as he heard James' footsteps and then dropped the paperwork that he had been holding onto the table in the conference room. He pointed back at the door, following James from the room.

"What happened, James? Something did." Lyle studied his detective, seeing the strain that James was under.

James told him, rubbing at the back of his neck. He was puzzled as to why the men had not taken Gideon and Garnet away from Gorrie's home.

"I don't understand it, Lyle. I think that they were waiting for someone." James eyed Toryn who had approached them at Lyle's wave.

"What happened, James?" Toryn listened patiently as James repeated his words. "They're okay?"

"They are, for now. I don't understand what happened." James ran his hand through his hair, something that he had done repeatedly over the last hour.

"It is strange. The men are not talking?" Lyle suspected that they were refusing to.

"No, they're not. And they have not asked for lawyers as of yet." James walked away. He had other cases that he needed to work on and this one with Gideon and Garnet would need to stay on the back burner for now, as people would say.

Toryn watched him walk away, his thoughts troubled.

"He needs some time off, Lyle. Make sure that he takes it." Toryn walked away, leaving Lyle nodding before he followed James.

Gideon wrapped an arm around Garnet as they sat on the wicker loveseat on the back deck. Gorrie eyed them before Belle poked him and pointed to Garnet's hand and the ring on it. He shared a looked with his wife before turning to his brother.

"Gideon? Let's pray for you two. Then, you can tell us exactly why you're here." Gorrie grinned at his brother before his head was bowed and he was praying for him.

Gideon appreciated his brother's prayers. They had been raised in a praying family, prayers coming as easily as they breathed.

Garnet studied the couple across from her, realizing that she was now part of a large family. She was scared somewhat at that but felt Gideon's arm tightening around her once more.

"Gideon? Who were those men?" Belle's soft voice broke through the stillness.

"I don't know, Belle. I really don't know. It was strange, though, the way that they just stayed there. They were waiting for someone to appear or for further orders. I'm sorry that you two were threatened." Gideon was contrite at that but was not sure how to continue.

"They were waiting for someone, Gideon." Garnet's voice was thoughtful. "I want to know who and why. How do we determine that?"

"It is difficult to do, Garnet. I am not sure that we have enough information to do that." Gorrie's voice was calm even as his thoughts raced. He was a private investigator and wanted to help his brother. "Let's call a family meeting with everyone, including the kids. They sometimes have an insight into people and events that we don't have." Gorrie grinned at his brother. "But there is other news?"

Gideon grinned at his brother before he reached for Garnet's hand. He lifted it to show the ring.

"I know that you'll say it's too soon, but we love one another and are planning on getting married." Gideon dropped a kiss on Garnet's cheek.

"Congratulations." Gorrie and Belle were on their feet to hug the couple before they sat back down. Gorrie shared a look with Belle. "How soon?"

Garnet stared at Gideon, reading the answer in his eyes.

"We don't want to wait too long. I have no family to invite. At least, I don't think that I do. I left home when I was younger and never contacted any family members." She paled. "Are they the ones after us?"

Gorrie's hand paused as he reached for his coffee mug. He drew out a pen and notepad.

"Let me have their name and what information that you can. I'll track them down and see what is going on." Gorrie's pen scratched across the paper. "I'll work on this but we also have a friend that we'll reach out to."

Gideon nodded, knowing who Gorrie meant.

"When do we get together?" Gideon turned to Belle, knowing that she would host the meeting. They had the biggest property and quite often did that.

"Tonight. We'll do a potluck, Gideon, just as always. We haven't had one in about a month." Her head turned as she heard the door. "The kids are here."

Amy and Abel appeared on the deck, sunburned and tousled. They squealed in delight to see their uncle and rushed to hug him and then hug Garnet. Without her knowing it, Garnet had become a large presence in the young teens' lives. They were delighted to see her.

"Uncle Gideon? Are you okay?" Eleven-year-old Abel was worried about his uncle.

"I am, Abel. We're having a meal here tonight. Are you coming?" He grinned as his nephew hugged him again. "I take it that's a yes."

Gideon walked Garnet to her door, reaching to kiss her as they stood on the front porch. His forehead rested against hers. He was deeply worried about her, feeling danger around them. They just could not see the danger or who it was that was after her and after him because of her.

“We need to make some plans, love.” Gideon was sorry that their special day had been damaged by the events.

“We will, Gideon. I don’t want a fancy wedding. It’s not the same without my parents and brother here. I’m not too sure about marrying into such a big family.” She smirked as he stared at her and then began to laugh.

Gideon reached to kiss her again, whispering a prayer for protection in her ear.

“We are a big happy family. They’ll just assimilate you into their group.” Gideon walked away at last, not happy that he had to.

Chapter 17

Running for her car the next morning, Garnet's breath was in gasps as she struggled to hit the right button on her key fob. She could hear the pounding footsteps behind her as she reached the car and wrenched for the door handle. Garnet pulled open the door, ready to jump inside. She just didn't make it. Arms wrapped around her and pulled her away from the open door.

A scream rising in her throat was stifled as one of the arms moved and a hand was clapped over her mouth. She was dragged towards the edge of the parking lot of the diner. For once, there were no cars coming or going. Garnet struggled to release herself, prevented from doing that as the arms were just too strong for her.

The man's fist came back and landed against her temple. Garnet slumped in his arms as her eyes closed. He hurriedly looked around before he dragged her into the bushes. Rope appeared in his hands as he worked quickly to bind her hands and feet. A gag was slapped across her face and tied almost too tightly around her face. Her body was hauled deeper into the bush and just dumped on the cool, damp ground.

The man walked from the area, his hands wiping on his jeans. He reached for the keys that Garnet had dropped and headed for her car. He waved at his accomplice and then drove away, heading for a nearby wrecking company that was owned by his employer. Her car was hidden deep on the lot, other cars piled up around it. To all extents and purposes, Garnet had left town.

Gideon stepped back from Garnet's front door late that afternoon. He was frowning. Garnet had told him that she would be there at that time, that she was working all day. He could not understand why she was not answering. Sudden fear had him running around the house searching and then heading for the garage. He peered inside and his heart fell. Her car was missing.

Walking back towards the front of the house as quickly as he could, Gideon pulled out his phone. He turned it over and over before he dialled a number.

"James? Garnet isn't home and she should be. Her car is missing as well." Gideon could hear the surprised tone in James' voice. "Yes, we were meeting tonight to make some plans. I should tell you that we are engaged." He grinned for a moment at the congratulations shot his way. "But that doesn't explain where she is. She promised that she would be here as she was working."

James was on his feet, heading to find Toryn.

"Toryn? Do you have a key to Garnet's home?" James' question had Toryn on his feet.

"I do. At home. Why?" Toryn was on his own feet, walking from the building with James.

"She's missing. She was to be at home but she's not. Gideon has searched outside and her car is gone."

"Gone? Okay, let me grab the keys and then I'll meet you there." Toryn was greatly troubled as he sat in his car before he reached for a radio, asking that an all points bulletin be put out for Garnet.

Slaney stared at Toryn as he reached for the keys to the house before she reached for her shoes, tugging them on. She was going with Toryn whether he wanted her to or not. He simply hugged her, knowing that Slaney's heart was sore for Garnet.

James walked slowly around the house. Responding officers had to literally force Gideon from the house and to the street. He stood and leaned against one of the patrol vehicles, his eyes watching the search that was going on. He also watched as Toryn approached an officer and handed over the keys before Toryn headed for James.

Gideon felt a hand on his arm and turned, not surprised to find Slaney beside him.

"Slaney?"

"It's okay, Gideon. I need to be here with you. Which of your family do you want?" Slaney had also taken it upon herself to call the church prayer chain lead and start the prayers for Garnet and also for their beloved pastor.

"Thank you, Slaney. The prayer chain is working?" He gave a brief grin.

"It is. And I want to know which of your family to call. You need one of them with you. At least one." Slaney's phone was out, her fingers poised to make that call.

Gideon looked past her, a frown on his face for a moment before his face cleared.

“It’s okay. Glynna’s here.” Gideon reached to hug his youngest sister. “Glynna?”

“God told me to find you. You weren’t at the church or your home. This is the only place that I could think of. What happened?” Glynna’s concern coloured her face as she stared up at the brother who had done his best to protect all of his siblings and had served as peacemaker more than once.

“Garnet is missing. We were to meet tonight for a meal and then to make our plans. She isn’t here.” Gideon’s face sobered and the two ladies could see the tears in his eyes.

Glynna simply reached to hug her brother. She had sent out a text to the others in the family, just letting them know that something was going on and that she would update as she could.

Gideon struggled with his emotions. It wasn’t how the night was to go, not by his and Garnet’s plans. He knew that God had plans for them and that this was likely a part of them. It was at times like that that is was so difficult to trust.

James turned away from the house. They had searched it carefully, seeing that Garnet had been there at some point. Her desk was laid out for her to work. Only, she was not there. He spoke with one of the techs.

“Janie, can we track her phone?”

“We can. I’ve already asked for that, knowing that you would.” Janie looked around. “She hasn’t been here since morning, I think. Her coffee cup is in the sink. The bread and toaster are still out. That doesn't make a lot of sense with the neatness in the rest of the house."

"No, it doesn't make sense. Get me your preliminary findings when you can. I know that you have a huge backlog."

"We do, but she's a missing person in the midst of a criminal investigation. We'll do what we can."

James walked away to find Toryn. That man turned from where he stood at the back of the yard, a hand resting against the wooden fence.

"James?"

"She was here at some point this morning. Where she is now? We don't know. Janie's started a search of her phone locations."

"That will help. Who's with Gideon?"

"Slaney. Glynna showed up as well. I haven't had a chance to speak with her to find out why she showed up."

"We'll get there." Toryn walked away at last, leaving James to stare up at the sky, asking, no begging, for help.

Chapter 18

Night fell with no sign of Garnet. The search had expanded with no one admitting to having seen her. The story made the local newscast. The woman from the book store stared at the television screen before she reached for her phone, calling the number that had been displayed. Garnet had been in her store late that morning but she had no idea where she had gone.

James reached for the message on his desk the next morning. He would need to head that way. He frowned before he rose from his chair and tapped at the map of the town that hung on his wall. His finger traced the area around the book store before his face paled.

Running for his car, James simply reached for his radio and asked for help. They would need to search the area around that parking lot. He prayed that Garnet was there and was well but he was afraid for her.

Standing in the parking lot, James was deep in conversation with a patrol officer. He turned in a circle, searching for where Garnet might be hiding. He didn't think that she had left town. Garnet would not have done that to Gideon.

His eyes landed on the group of trees and underbrush at the edge of the park. He gave a shout and began to run towards it. An officer who had been walking towards him paused and then turned and sprinted that way as well. They frantically began to search the area, shoving aside branches and tall weeds.

The officer gave a loud shout and was then on his knees, a hand reaching to turn Garnet to her side. He felt for a pulse, looking up with a nod as James stood with his hand on the man's shoulder.

James immediately turned to send another officer to call for aid. He was then on his knees on Garnet's other side, reaching with a knife to cut away her bonds and the gag. He frowned, knowing that she had been there for at least twenty-four hours.

Garnet's face was pale, more pale than James thought that he had seen. Tear tracks marked her cheeks and there was evidence that she had struggled to free herself without any help. James shrugged out of his jacket and draped it over her in an effort to keep her warm. He didn't know if it would help. He was on his feet as he heard the sirens and then the hurried movements of the paramedics as they swiftly headed his way. All he could do at this point was pray for her and for Gideon. He had spotted the ring on her finger.

Gideon looked around from where he had been sitting in the sanctuary, on the very first pew. He was on his feet as Toryn approached him, fear on his face.

"Toryn?" Gideon could barely get out the words. He was afraid for his lady, not sleeping the night before but spending the time in prayer instead.

"Come with me, Gideon. We have Garnet." Toryn's hand went out to steady Gideon.

"You do? Is she alive?" Gideon held his breath, his eyes on his friend.

"She is. She's at the hospital right now. James and some officers found her." Toryn's hand went up. "Let's get you to your lady and then we'll talk." He nodded at the board chair as he approached.

Paul's hand reached to rest on Gideon's shoulders.

"Go and be with your lady, Gideon. I know that it's Bible study night. I'll run it. You need to be with Garnet for now. The board is well aware of your feelings for one another. We'll work through what we need to. Call me when you can get an update to me."

"Thank you, Paul." Gideon's steps were hesitant until he gathered his strength. He looked up for a moment, a silent prayer for his lady.

Gideon found it very hard to wait to be taken to his lady. He had been through it too many times with his congregation and friends. James had appeared, nodded at him, and then disappeared into the area where the rooms were.

Feeling a hand on his shoulder, Gideon looked up. His brother, Galway, and sister, Gemma, were there, just to wait with him. It was what his family did for one another. It was usually Gideon who was the one providing prayers and comfort. This time? He was the one receiving it.

"Any word?" Galway looked around, nodding at the people whom he knew.

"Not yet. Toryn didn't say much. Not that he could. He just said that Garnet was safe and alive." He squinted at them. "Who called you?"

"James. He said you needed us. He was right. You do need your family. I had the day off and Gemma just took the time." He grinned briefly at his brother. "It's hard to receive when you're used to giving."

"It is. I preach that all the time, don't I?" Gideon sat back, his siblings on either side of him. "Where are the others?"

"At work and praying for you, bro." Galway knew that for a fact. It was how they were raised. "The kids are gathering at Gorrie's, even the little ones. They are planning of spending time in prayer as well. Mom and Dad would be so proud of them."

"They would be. I wish that they were here but they can't be, can they?" Gideon was on his feet as a nurse approached him. He could hear Galway and Gemma behind him as he walked towards where his lady was.

The physician turned as the trio approached.

"Gideon? She's been awake and given her statement. She's sleeping right now." He looked down at Garnet. "She was outside overnight. From what James said, she was bound and gagged and was unable to free herself." His hand rested gently on one of Garnet's wrists which was wrapped in a light bandage. "Other than that, she seems to be in good health." His hand rested on Gideon's shoulder as he passed him. Gideon was a well-loved figure in their community. None of them could understand why this was happening to Gideon.

Galway and Gemmas waited near the door, their eyes on their brother. They shared a look before Galway's phone was out to send out a group text to let the family know that Gideon was with his lady and that they really didn't know a lot.

Garnet shifted on the stretcher, rousing somewhat as she felt Gideon's kiss on her cheek. A smile briefly crossed her face before she drifted off to a normal sleep, her hand tight in her beloved's.

Chapter 19

Gideon rose from the chair that he had planted beside Garnet's bed and stretched. He squinted at his watch. It was late evening and to now, Garnet had not really roused. He would need to leave soon but didn't want to. Gideon rested a hand on Garnet's face, a sober look on his face. He loved this lady so much but he had no idea what to do to protect her.

Gideon stood for a moment before he walked away, heading for the elevator. He paused as he saw Galway waiting for him.

"Gideon? How is Garnet?" Galway looked past his brother towards the room that he had just exited.

"She's sleeping. She has roused every once in a while but hasn't completely roused. I worry about her, Galway. How do I keep her safe?"

"Stop doing God's work for Him, bro. He's watching out for her. You and I both know that sometimes things are difficult to understand. I don't need to tell you that." Galway pointed towards where he had parked. "Come on. Brenna wants you to come home with me. She's worried about you and I would like to do something to relieve some of that worry."

"Thanks, Galway. That helps. I'm not sure that I'll be good company."

"Doesn't matter. You're family and that's all that counts. She'll have a meal ready for you. The kids are asleep." Galway and Brenna had two girls, both under the age of ten, who adored their uncle and their uncle adored them.

"That's okay. They are young and it is late." Gideon grew pensive, not sure what he was thinking other than that he was praying.

"What did they say, Gid?" Galway's fingers tapped at the steering wheel, not quite sure what to ask his brother. None of them had been through anything like this.

"Not a lot, unfortunately. She has no one to speak for her so I asked to do that. They agreed, seeing as we are engaged." Gideon sighed, his eyes closing. He was fatigued beyond what he had ever experienced. He knew that it was only by God's strength that he was still on his feet. "She was out overnight, so that is a concern. They'll keep her in at least until tomorrow. I'm afraid, Galway. I'm afraid that I'll lose her." Gideon blinked back the tears that he would not shed.

"We know that, Gid." Galway parked in his driveway and then shifted on his seat to study his younger brother. "We have never gone through something like this. God is allowing this, as you know. He knows the path that He has chosen for you to walk. Out of all of us, you are the one best suited for this, if any of us could be."

Gideon was nodding. It was not the first time that he and his older brother had spoken of what people were facing and how to cope. They both had agreed that without God, it was not possible to truly cope with danger.

Gideon walked slowly through Galway's home, heading for the kitchen. Brenna turned from where she had been dishing up bowls of soup and simply hugged her brother-in-law. He clung to her for a moment before he stepped back, reaching for a mug to pour himself some tea. He leaned against the counter, his mug of tea in his hand. He studied Brenna and then Galway.

"The girls are asleep?" His voice was not his usual strong, vibrant one. They could hear the fatigue and worry and stress in it.

"They are. They wanted to stay up and see you but they were falling asleep. Go on through, Gideon, and say your good nights to them." Brenna watched as he watched away, his shoulders stooped. This was not the Gideon that they knew and loved.

"He's hurting, Brenna." Galway wrapped his wife in his arms. "And we can't make it better for him. He's always been there for us."

"He has. He's played that role for so many years. Now, it's his turn to receive our help. I'm just not sure that he will." Brenna moved away to set the bowls of soup on the table for her husband and brother-in-law before she set a plate of freshly sliced bread down as well. Brenna paused, her thoughts muddled before she began to pray for Gideon. She sensed that he was only starting out on this adventure and that if it was like his friends, he could very well face life and death.

Gideon paused in the hallway outside of the girls' bedrooms. He peeked through the open doors, seeing that the girls were indeed asleep. He walked quietly into each room, dropping a kiss on each of their heads and prayed for each of them. Gideon loved his nieces dearly and was just so afraid that the danger that he seemed to be in would affect them. He didn't know if he could live with himself if one of them was harmed.

Galway walked towards his brother, a hand out to draw him away from the hallway and towards the kitchen.

"Brenna has food ready for us, Gideon. It's just soup and fresh bread. You need to eat. I know you. You spent the time in prayer and fasting. I'll get you home when you're done." Galway was afraid suddenly for his brother, dread wafting through him.

"Thank you, Galway. Your wife has a giving heart as do you." Gideon sank into a chair at the kitchen table, his head landing in his hands. "I'm sorry. I think that I am too dangerous to know right at the moment."

"That may well be, Gideon, but you are family." Brenna hugged him as best she could and then sat at the table as well, a mug of tea in front of her. "We'll deal with what we have to. It's just that we didn't expect this to happen with you."

"I didn't either." Gideon spooned his soup into his mouth, not really conscious of what he was doing. "How well do you know Garnet?"

"Not that well. I have wanted to get to know her better. The kids all love her, no matter what their ages are." Brenna shared a look with Galway. "Gideon, I know that you love her and that she loves you. What are your plans?"

Gideon shrugged. Their declared love for one another was just too new. To have Garnet disappear like that had frightened him. He was afraid that she would disappear on him and he would never find her again. Gideon sighed to himself. His brother was right. He was doing God's job, that of worrying about how to keep his lady love safe. A yawn caught him unawares. Galway's hand on his arm drew him to his feet and to a guest room. Gideon stretched out on top of the bed and was asleep before his head had even settled on the pillow.

Brenna turned from where she was clearing away the meal and walked into Galway's hug. She could hear his prayer for his brother and his lady. Brenna was afraid for the couple, more afraid than she could have imagined to have ever been.

Chapter 20

Rousing slightly, Garnet kept her eyes closed. She shivered from the fever that she was fighting and snuggled down further under the covers. She could hear light footsteps around her and had to keep herself from jumping in fear as fingers wrapped around her wrist for a few moments. Garnet strained to hear and then understand where she was but just could not. Hearing the footsteps leaving her side, she looked around through slitted eyes, surprised to find herself in a hospital room. It was not where she had expected to be.

Her eyes closed again as she tried to think what had happened to her. Her head was pounding too hard for her thoughts to be clear. Garnet froze for a moment, sensing evil around her that was growing stronger with each beat of her heart. She heard soft motion around her but refused to open her eyes. She just didn't want to see what was waiting. She felt a presence stop by her bed and the sense of evil and danger grew even stronger. Garnet knew that she was just not strong enough to leap from the bed and run.

The noise stopped for a few seconds and Garnet waited with a growing sense of terror and danger. She felt something cross her face and a hand land on her chest. She struggled to pull at the pillow that covered her face but she was just not strong enough to fight off the hands that held her down. Her arms flailed at the man, her movements growing weaker and weaker until she was still.

Garnet didn't hear the shout that resounded through the hospital room. The darkness had taken over her vision and she was lost to consciousness. She didn't hear the loud yell or the sound of running footsteps.

Don tackled Garnet's assailant, pulling him away from the bed and then to the floor. One of his team, Thomas, was helping him as they struggled to contain the man and hold him to the floor. Mark, the paramedic on Don's team, was around them and bending over Garnet, tossing the pillow that still covered her face towards a chair. He was afraid that they were too late. He breathed in a sigh of relief when he found a faint pulse, despite his frantic efforts to try and revive her. He heard the running footsteps as nurses appeared at his side, a physician running after them, his long white lab coat flapping around his legs.

Mark stepped back as he watched the hurried movements of the medical staff, listening to their conversation as he did so. He knew that Paul had planted himself at the door, not letting anyone in except for medical staff. He watched as Don and Thomas still struggled with the man. He walked to the door and stared down the hallway to where he saw Caleb and Joshua standing, each facing opposite directions. Gideon was behind them, his back to the wall. Mark could see the strained, worried look on his face. He walked towards the trio, not sure what to say.

"Mark?" Caleb's voice was quiet, a contrast to the yell that had split the quiet of the late-night hospital stillness and roused the patients, some of those who had wandered into the corridor to try and understand what was happening to disturb them. The hospital security was herding them back into their rooms.

Mark shook his head. He was not ready to say what had happened, not yet. He watched the measured, stern footsteps of the police officers who had responded to the call for them. James walked past the four men, nodding at them. He paused in the doorway of the room, Paul watching him closely.

"Paul?" James kept his voice low. "What happened?"

"Someone tried to suffocate Garnet. I'm not sure how he got in. The hospital was locked for the night."

"They always find ways to get in." James walked into the room, standing to one side as he watched the officers pulling the handcuffed man to his feet and then shoving him out into the hallway. He then turned to the subdued bustle around the bed. He walked closer to the bed, concern for Garnet filling his mind as well as trying to determine who the man was.

The physician turned away at last, confident that they had revived Garnet and that she would live. It had been close and they had struggled to bring her back to life. He nodded towards the corner of the room and walked that way, James at his side.

"She's okay?" James held his breath as the physician hesitated for a moment.

"She will be. The quick work by that man saved her life. It was almost too late." The physician rubbed at his face. "Who is she?"

"Garnet? She's engaged to our minister, Gideon. I'm not sure that it's gotten out that much."

"She is?" The physician, Rob Rogers by name, was a member of Gideon's church. "This must be new. I wasn't aware that he was dating anyone."

"It is new. They're involved in one of those adventures that our friends seem to think that they need." James shared a look with Don, who was standing near Garnet. "He's out in the hallway. We need to get him in here."

"And we will. Just give us a few moments with Garnet. Find out who ordered it. She might not survive the next attempt on her life. Find out why." Bob walked away, heading for the nurse's station to make his notes on Garnet's chart.

James sighed. That was what they were trying hard to do but it just didn't seem to be working out very well. His eyes found the ceiling as he begged God for the answer to what was going on. He didn't get a sense of relief that he usually did when he prayed. James sighed once more. This meant that he had a lot of work to do and he asked for the strength that he needed to continue. He also prayed for Garnet and her return to health.

Gideon shifted restlessly from foot to foot. He desperately wanted to be with his lady but understood that he had to wait. It was just so had to do that. His troubled thoughts turned to anxious prayers before he began to praise God. God was in control and knew the path that Gideon and Garnet were walking. He just didn't like that his lady was in danger.

Finally called to walk towards Garnet's room, Gideon moved that way, surrounded by Don's security team. Their attention was not on him or the room ahead of them. Their concentration was on the surrounding area. They knew that there was still danger out there and they were determined to protect both Gideon and Garnet.

Gideon paused for a moment at the entrance to the room, not sure what he would find. He looked up once more, asking for protection and relief from their danger. He nodded before he moved forward, his eyes on his lady and not on the ones who were in the room. His left hand landed on her cheek, feeling the line that fed oxygen to her body even as his other hand found hers.

Chapter 21

With a sober and sorrowful look on his face, Gideon stared down at the lady he loved. She was unconscious and not even aware that he was there. He drew in a deep breath, knowing that he would need to leave and ready to refuse to. He heard the noise and saw movement around him as the medical staff were working around him. He was also aware of Mark standing nearby and that Paul was still planted at the room door. Gideon had no idea where the other four men were but he knew that they would be around the floor somewhere.

James walked away at last, frustrated that he could not speak with Garnet. He had been told that they had no idea when that would be possible. Walking through the police department building not long after that, he looked for one of the officers who had brought in Garnet's assailant.

"Who is it?" James watched the frustration that crossed the officer's face.

"He has no identification on him. He's not talking and hasn't asked for a lawyer as yet. And he's not in the system to identify him that way." The officer was frustrated. Gideon had been a good friend to the force and that consideration for Gideon extended now to Garnet.

"I see. And we need him to do that, don't we?" James was frustrated as well. He yawned as he set his phone on his desk and then sat in his chair, his head buried in his hands. He had no idea where to go for now. James was swamped with cases and there just was not enough information to move forward with the investigation. It had to be set aside and that was not what he wanted to do.

Gideon paced his home late that night. Don had made sure that he had arrived home and then left, admonishing Gideon to lock himself into his house. What had happened to Garnet had shocked him deeply! He wanted to know why and who. James had called him not that long before. He had no idea who it was that was behind his trouble.

He finally turned to find his rest, his eyes closing without any conscious thought on his part. He slept but his sleep was troubled and filled with dreams of losing Garnet. On his feet in the early morning, Gideon dressed and then found his prayer corner. His head was bowed as tears flowed down his cheeks. Gideon felt broken in mind and soul.

Garnet had not awakened since the attempt on her life the night before. That concerned the medical staff. They could not assess her fully until she did. And they had no idea when that would happen. All they knew was that entrance to her room was severely restricted and a police officer was stationed at her door twenty-four hours a day. Anyone entering the room had been fully vetted and restricted to just a few. Don and his team were in and out, just as a secondary measure to her safety.

A day passed, a long, worrying day for all of Gideon's family. They fully supported Gideon, coming to stand beside him as he waited to see Garnet and just to be there if he needed to talk. That was what his family did.

No one saw the woman who stalked the waiting room and the hospital corridors, her eyes trained on Garnet's room and then on Gideon. She knew that he was well protected as was Garnet. She would find a way to reach them and when she did, Garnet would pay the price of avoiding her. Don watched her at one time, a frown on his face before he shook his head. He had no idea who she was but at the present time, she didn't seem to present a danger to either one of the couple.

Garnet began to rouse the next day, fighting the hands that held her still and the ones that keep the oxygen on her. She couldn't understand what was happening. She was disoriented and didn't know exactly where she was. All she knew what that she hurt and was fighting a fever.

Gideon paused in the doorway, his gaze following the activity around Garnet. The charge nurse for the floor had called him and asked him to come. He had dropped the papers that he had been reading and raced for the hospital. He walked forward to stand beside her bed, a hand reaching for hers. Gideon felt Garnet's hand gripping his hand even as she was still trying to rouse. He reached to kiss her forehead, finding her face turning towards him.

His attention on Garnet, he didn't see the woman who walked past the room door, her attention on him. Mark watched her from his post at the door, a frown on his face. His phone was out as he took a picture and sent it on to Don. He frowned once more at the text message that Don sent him before he tucked away his phone.

Garnet's eyes flickered open and closed before she stared around the room. A hospital room? What had she done that she couldn't remember doing? She felt a hand tighten on hers and frowned at it before she looked up at the tall handsome man standing beside her bed. She didn't recognize him right away.

"Garnet? Love? Are you okay?" Gideon's smile was tender as a hand rested on her cheek.

"Who are you?" Garnet felt safe in his presence even though she could not understand why.

"I'm Gideon. We're engaged, Garnet. It's okay. You were through a lot in the last few days." Gideon watched her carefully, a sympathetic look on his face and his love for her shining in his eyes.

"I have been. Why am I here?" Garnet felt herself beginning to panic even as James appeared. "Who are you?"

"I'm James, the investigator on your case. Everyone, please leave? I need to speak with Garnet." He watched, somewhat amused, as Garnet clung to Gideon and that Gideon was very reluctant to leave his lady.

Gideon stood outside of the hospital room, leaning against the wall opposite the door, his eyes on Garnet and James. He could see that Garnet was focused on him and not James. Paul and Thomas stood on either side of him, their eyes on the movement around them. This is when it could go very bad and do that very quickly.

Chapter 22

Pulling out his notepad, James waited for Garnet to look at him. Only she never did. He smiled as he turned for a moment to look towards Gideon. James needed Garnet to speak with him but it seemed obvious to everyone that she wouldn't do that. James walked towards the door and beckoned to Gideon.

"Gideon? We need you in here. I need to get Garnet's statement. She's not looking at me or ready to do that. You need to be in here." James' hand on his back shoved him back towards where Garnet was waiting, a hand out to grip Gideon's.

"Garnet? You do need to talk to James. Tell him what happened." Gideon lowered the side rail to the bed and sat beside her, wrapping an arm around her. He could feel the shuddering that wracked her body and realized that she was not only terrified but was running a high fever as well.

"I don't remember anything, Gideon. Not one thing. I remember being in church on Sunday and then waking up here this morning." She turned tortured eyes to James, blinking to try and bring moisture to the dryness that she felt in them.

"You can't remember anything, Garnet?" This is not what James wanted to hear. If she could not remember what had happened to her, then they could not solve the mystery surrounding her or protect her.

"Nothing. I'm sorry." Tears filled her eyes before her head was down on Gideon's shoulder and she slept.

Gideon watched her, just wanting to whisk her away somewhere that she would be safe but he couldn't do that. He needed to be back in his church office for a counselling session in just a little while. He rose and settled her back on the bed, pulling the covers up around her and then dropped a kiss on her forehead. Gideon walked away, his shoulders slumping for a moment.

James tucked his pen and notepad away into his shirt pocket. He watched Gideon walk away and then turned back to study Garnet. He sighed, something that he felt he was doing a lot and then walked away. He had other investigations that he needed to be at.

Gideon raised his head at last. It was early evening and he was fatigued. He knew part of that was not sleeping much over the last couple of days and then the worry about Garnet was weighing heavily on him. He had given the situation to God but he still worried about her. He could here Gemma telling him that he was doing God's job. He was on his feet, locking up his office, and heading for the outside door. He set the alarm for the church and then headed for his car. He paused for a moment, his eyes closing as he drew in some deep breaths. Gideon felt peace for a moment, the peace that only God could give.

Garnet had roused not long after Gideon had left. She was on her feet, finding her clothes and then creeping from the hospital. She walked towards her home, struggling to breathe, the fever causing her to shiver despite the heat of the summer afternoon.

Finally reaching her house, she slumped to the front steps for a moment before she dragged herself to her feet and then unlocked her door to enter and then to lock it behind her. She headed for her bedroom, knowing that she needed a shower and then clean clothes. Garnet grabbed a bottle of water from the fridge on her way by. Showered and in clean clothes, she simply crawled into her bed and slept.

Gideon stood and stared at the charge nurse who was shaking her head at him. He looked past her, seeing Paul walking towards him, a grim look on that man's face.

"What do you mean, she's gone?" Gideon shook his head. There was no way that she would have left the hospital. At least, he didn't think that she would. He almost ran from the building, heading for Garnet's home. His prayers were raising that she was there. Gideon paused at the door, a hand raised to knock before he dropped it. He had no idea if she was there. If she was, would he be disturbing her?

His hand raised again as he knocked at her door. He waited and then repeated it. He heard stumbling footsteps at last and then the door cracked open. Gideon could see one eye peeking around the door at him.

"It had to be you, didn't it?" Garnet was grumpy and showed it. She pulled the door open further and let Gideon in. "Don't you work?"

Gideon stared at her for a moment before he simply wrapped her into a hug. She stiffened for a moment before she almost melted against him, her arms hugging him tightly.

"I'm scared, Gideon. I am so scared." She sniffed as she tried to control her tears. "Who is doing that? I want to know that."

"I know that you do, love. So do I." He seated her at the kitchen table and reached for the kettle to make them each a cup of tea. Once it was ready, he set their mugs on the table and then seated himself beside her, wrapping her into his arms. "God is in control, even though it might not seem like He is. He wants only the best for us. Sometimes, His best takes us through trouble and danger. That is when our faith comes in. We have to trust in something and Someone that we can't see or feel. It's hard."

"It is very hard, isn't it?" Garnet leaned harder against Gideon. "Gideon, are you sure?"

"Am I sure? About what?" Gideon tilted his head to study the lady he loved more than his own life.

"About marrying me. We just sort of jumped into it."

"We did, but I am sure. You're the one I was waiting for all my life." Gideon reached to kiss her. "We'll work through this, love. Right now, you need to heal." He kissed her again and then rose and headed for his own home. He heard the door lock behind him. Gideon just didn't hear the thud as Garnet's body hit the floor and the sobs that shook her body in a violent manner.

Gareth was seated on his brother's front porch, answering the nudge from God that he needed to be with his brother. Annie had sent him, knowing that the siblings were close and that each one would follow the nudges that God gave to them.

"Gideon? You okay?" Gareth was on his feet to hug his brother and then to stand with his hands planted on Gideon's shoulders.

"No, I'm not, Gareth. And I don't know how to heal. My lady is in danger and I don't know how to protect her from." Gideon brushed at the tears on his cheeks. His emotions had finally spilled over.

"Inside, Gid. We'll pray this through. And I want to work on this with you. All of us do, including the kids. Gorrie's planning a meeting tomorrow as it's Saturday. Are you free?"

"I have a counselling session in the morning but I am after lunch. Annie needs to reach out to Garnet. She may have a hard time convincing her to come."

"I doubt that. She's already reached out, I guess just after you left. She headed Garnet's way. She didn't want your lady on her own." Gareth studied his bother. "And Aaron is with Gorrie."

Chapter 23

With Annie's arm around her, Garnet approached Gorrie's home the next morning. She had protested that she should not be there at a family gathering. Annie had simply hugged her and told her that she was family. Garnet had been chosen by Gideon and the whole family was welcoming her in. They had often wondered who Gideon would choose. Annie decided that Garnet was just right for Gideon.

Swarmed by all the children and young teens, Garnet's face lit up with laughter. She allowed herself to be led away, the adults watching with amused smiles on their faces. Annie followed the group, laughing softly as Garnet was pulled down into the midst.

Gareth's arm went around his wife, an amused look on his own face.

"She is loved by our kids, isn't she?"

"She is. Just as Gideon is. He's been the fun uncle to them all. Aaron has often asked why he doesn't have a lady."

"He does now. And they are just right for each other." He looked around. "Where are we working?"

"The office. Belle has already set up in there." Annie waited for Gareth to move, content just to watch the activity in the sun room.

Gareth bit at his lip for a moment, watching Garnet once more.

“Let’s head that way then.” Gareth walked away, leaving Annie to follow after a few moments.

Gideon appeared at last, his counselling session finished. His first thought was to look for Garnet. He found her deep in reading some paperwork, her feet tucked up under her as she curled up in a corner of the couch. He sat beside her with his arm coming around her. He felt Garnet shift to lean against him without taking her attention from the papers.

“What are you reading, love?” Gideon waited patiently for Garnet to speak.

“Some information that Galway handed me. It is interesting but I have no idea what to think of it.” She sighed as she handed it over. “Maybe you’ll see something that I am missing.”

Gideon nodded as he took the papers, reading through them. He frowned. What was Galway looking for with this? He looked up to see Galway sitting across from him, a grin on his face. “Galway?”

“Gideon?” Galway nodded at the paperwork. “I found this information and I’m not sure what to think of it. What are your thoughts?”

“To tell you the truth? I’m not sure, Galway. What were you thinking?”

Galway shrugged, hearing conversation around him. He had no idea how that material had found its way to his attention, other than it was God. He didn’t know what to do with it.

Gideon pulled out his phone in frustration. It had not stopped chiming. He frowned at it before his face cleared. Emma Finlay, a friend from Riverville, had sent a text. She had been told that he was in the middle of an adventure. Could she and her husband, Abe, meet with them tomorrow after church? He sent back a quick text agreeing. Emma had a business where she found information and people that no one else seemed to be able to find.

"Emma's been in touch, Galway. We'll meet tomorrow." Gideon's eyes were on Garnet who had looked up at him.

"Emma? Is she from Riverville? If she is, then I know her." Garnet snuggled closer to Gideon, finding comfort and peace in how he held her.

"She is. They're heading this way tomorrow after church." Gideon bit at his lip. "I said that it was okay. I should have asked you first."

Garnet shrugged, knowing that Gideon had acted out of fear and love for her.

"It's okay, Gideon. Where were we?" She pulled the papers back from his grip and read through them once more. "Galway, who are these people? I don't know them."

"They run a large real estate company here in Oak City. There have always been rumours that they are not legitimate but no one has ever been able to prove it. But that doesn't explain how they would know you. You're not from here." Galway had been puzzled by that. "Remind me, Garnet. What actually do you do for work?"

"I'm a free-lance copywriter, working from home. It doesn't matter where I live. I access everything on line." Garnet looked down at the paperwork again before she looked up at him. "I have never heard of this company. I don't do copy writing for real estate firms."

"I see." Galway was on his feet, returning in a few moments with more papers. "Take a look at these. We found this information but we weren't sure what to make of it." He handed it over to Garnet, Gideon reaching to turn her hand so that he could read it over with her.

Garnet frowned at this new batch of papers that she was holding. She was exhausted in more ways than one but was determined to solve whatever it was. It was not fair to Gideon, she decided. He had been drawn into whatever was going on against his will. Or had he? She turned her face to study him, watching as he read through the paperwork. Garnet knew that she loved this tall handsome man who wanted to protect her so badly.

"Garnet? Do you recognize this name?" Gideon looked up at that point, his eyes in turn studying her. "Garnet?"

Garnet shook herself and then stared down at the paperwork.

"What name? That one? No, I don't think that I do." She read the paragraph about him. "It says that he's a copywriter as well and for the same company. We don't know who all works for the company. It's not how it works. We don't usually work on teams but as individuals. I think that they have a division that does have teams. I was never offered a position there. I had made it very clear that I worked from outside of the office only and that on my own." She sighed. "You want to know who I've worked for/"

"No, we don't need to know that. I think that would be considered confidential." Gorrie spoke from where he had seated himself nearby. "James would find out that information, I'm sure, and then approach you." Gorrie was tired. He had not been sleeping well, he was that worried about his brother and his lady. "Gideon? Who would be after you?"

Gideon nodded. Gorrie had asked the very question that he had been asking himself. He reached for his shirt pocket, pulling out a paper.

"These people. I haven't given any names that I can't. There are not a lot of people." He shared a look with his brothers and then with his three sisters who had gathered nearby. "And yes, I passed it on to Emma."

Chapter 24

The next morning, Gideon stood at the front of the sanctuary, his eyes on his sermon notes. His hands clenched the pulpit tightly. He was afraid and deeply so that morning. He could feel evil in the church, something that he normally did not feel. His head raised as he searched the congregation. Gideon found Garnet where she was seated at the back of the church. He nodded to himself. James was on one side of her, Don and his wife on the other side. He knew that Don's team was scattered throughout the sanctuary, not sitting together as they usually did.

His eyes raised to the ceiling for a moment before he nodded. He began to speak, his words sounding loud and sure in the silence, not at all how he was feeling inside. Gideon knew that this was one time that God was speaking through him and he had to let him.

"God is our shield and protector. He hides us in the hollow of His hand and in the cleft of the rock. He covers us with His hand." Gideon paused as he saw the nods that followed his words. "It doesn't mean that we don't face danger or illness or injury. We do. God doesn't promise that we will have an eventless life. Instead, He has promised to never leave us or forsake us. He has provided a Comforter for us so that we know He is there. Whatever we face? God has already walked that path before us and laid it out. He knows how we will react and how we will respond. All we can do is leave our hand in His and walk forward with confidence that He is in control."

Gideon stood at the open doorway for a moment, watching as the last few stragglers were leaving the parking lot. He was well aware that James and Don were still there, standing beside Garnet in a protective manner. He felt a hand on his back and turned to wrap Garnet into a hug. He loved this lady but he could feel the approaching dark of danger and didn't want to lose her. He had had to fight out this battle over the night before, releasing Garnet to God's care. It had hurt to do that. Gideon wanted to be the one who saved her.

"All set, Gideon?" Garnet waited for him to speak.

"I am. I just need to close up my office and then we can leave. Abe said that he'd be at my place in about an hour. That gives you time to change if you want to."

"I brought some clothes with me, thinking that would work. If it doesn't, we can stop by my home."

Don walked away with Gideon as James stood beside Garnet. Neither man wanted to let the two be on their own. They could feel the danger around the two, not the first time that they had felt that around endangered couples.

Gideon stood for a moment, his keys in his hands. He turned to Don, his mouth opening and then closing.

"You want to know how to proceed?" Don waited for Gideon to nod. "You're off tomorrow.

We'll meet. Try and see if Garnet can make it. She said that you're meeting with Abe and Emma this afternoon."

"We are. Emma has information for us. I'll get her to pass it on to your team so that you can work on it. Abe will also have suggestions from a security standpoint. We'll talk, Don. Right now, I need to find my lady."

Garnet turned from the counter where she had been working on their meal. Her hands rubbed at the sides of her blue jeans. She turned as she felt a hand on her arm and hugged Emma. Emma was a hugger, not ashamed that she was. Abe reached to hug her as well, assessing her from the standpoint of protecting someone. He shared a look with Emma, seeing the concern that flickered in his wife's eyes.

"Emma? Abe? I'm glad that you are here. Maybe we can figure this all out." Garnet set the salads on the table, Emma's hands reaching to help.

"We'll see what we can do for you and Gideon. It's not the first time that we've had such a limited amount of information to work with." Emma sat, her hand reaching to squeeze Garnet's. "Let's eat and then spend time in prayer. Abe and his team have been working out what you could do to stay safe. He's reached out to Don and also Richard from Elmton."

"I thought that you would, Abe. It's who you are and what you do." Abe studied the couple as they ate and talked, laughter sprinkling through the words.

The meal finished and the debris left over tidied away, Abe led them in a time of prayer. Gideon felt grateful for the way that Abe had brought them right into God's presence. He felt a semblance of peace coming over him. His hand tightened on Garnet's, finding hers tightening back on his.

"Okay, Emma. What do you have?" Gideon went right to the heart of why Abe and Emma were there.

Emma rose and retrieved the file folders that she had dropped onto the countertop. She sat, her eyes on the folders before she began to speak.

"Gideon? Garnet? I have found some information that I need to share with you. Once we've discussed it, Abe wants to speak about security measures. He and the rest of the team had sat down and come up with some plans. He has also talked with Don, who says that he is meeting with you two tomorrow."

"That's right. Don asked that we meet tomorrow. We want this over, just as we did for everyone else who has been involved in something like this." Gideon was at a loss, however, to know how to proceed or even what to think.

"We'll get you there, Gideon. You may need to stand back from your church for a while. They support you, have no doubt about that. Garnet? Your work is secure? No one can find you through it?"

"They might if they hack into the system. We're supposed to be very secure but I have never felt completely comfortable with it. I have been thinking of looking for something else to do." Garnet rubbed her hand on the tabletop. "Do you know anyone who could check into that?"

Abe and Emma shared a look. Their team mate, Micah, might be able to but they had a friend who was an ethical hacker. They would put Noah in touch with Garnet. In fact, it would be a good idea, Abe decided. Garnet needed to hear Noah and his wife, Rowan's, story.

"I know of someone. I'll reach out to him, Garnet. He is an ethical hacker and would be more than willing to help." Abe reached for his phone to send off a text to Noah, not surprised at his instant response. "He's busy tomorrow but could meet with you and Gideon on Tuesday night, if that works."

"It does for me. Gideon has a meeting that night." Garnet drew in a deep breath. "Tell him to come and meet with me. I need to know for sure if my work is the reason we're going through this."

Chapter 25

Tuesday night came all too soon and not soon enough to ease Garnet's mind. She was unsure about meeting two more people. She was an introvert and had been meeting too many people for her liking. She wanted to go back to the life that she had had before all this but that would never happen. Garnet stared down at her ring, her thoughts muddled as she did so. Gideon loved her and while not putting any pressure on her, had expressed his desire that they marry soon. He was that worried about her on her own. Garnet had not made any comment about that. She was missing her family at that point, wanting her mother to discuss this with her.

Turning back to the door, she walked into Gideon's hug, hearing his prayer for her as she did so. She looked past him at the couple who were walking up to the front porch. She shook her head. No, she decided, she didn't know them even though she felt that they were friends.

"Garnet, love? This is Noah and his wife, Rowan. He's the ethical hacker that Abe and I mentioned."

"Hi. Welcome to my home." Garnet was wrapped in hugs which surprised her. Afterwards, she decided that it was becoming a habit, to be hugged in greeting.

"Garnet? It is good to meet you although I think we would prefer it to be on a different level." Noah grinned at her. "Don't worry. We know what danger is like. We've been through that as has a number of our friends, including my own cousin. Now, can we go inside? Someone is out here watching you two."

Garnet turned back to the house, pausing for a moment, a sense of terror and dread that almost drove her to her knees. She stiffened them before almost running inside. Gideon frowned at her before he followed her, stopping her when he wrapped her in his arms.

Seated in her home office, Garnet watched as Noah worked away on her computer. She trusted him, she decided, even though he was a stranger to her. She felt a hand touch hers and turned to Rowan. Rowan motioned towards the doorway, rising and following Garnet. Gideon watched his lady walk away, sorrow for the moment on his face. She was hurting and he could't make it better for her. They had talked daily, either in person or on the phone. Secrets, wishes, wants, hopes, and dreams had been shared between them. It had not surprised them how close what they wanted was. God had led them to one another.

Gideon turned his attention to Noah, seeing how intent his friend was on what he was investigating.

"Noah? Can you explain to Garnet exactly what you're doing? She will never ask for that but she needs to know."

Noah looked around, surprised to see that the ladies had left. He sighed. He tended to get lost in what he was doing and that would not work in this instance.

"I can. Where are they?" Noah looked around, not seeing their wives.

"I'll find them." Gideon rose, his socked feet whispering softly on the hardwood floor. He searched for the ladies, finally opening the back door. Garnet and Rowan were standing on the back deck, not speaking. Gideon frowned before he wrapped an arm around his lady. "Noah would like to speak with you, love. He wants to explain what he is doing."

Garnet turned her head, finding herself almost nose to nose with Gideon who had tilted his head to watch her face. He dropped a kiss on her cheek before turning her to walk back to the office. He could hear Rowan walking behind them. Garnet would never tell him but Rowan had shared a brief outline of what she and Noah had gone through. Garnet had been horrified to hear that Rowan had been stabbed and left for dead all those years ago.

"Noah? Here are the ladies. What do you have to tell Garnet?" Gideon's arm forced Garnet towards the desk. He could feel her resisting and frowned at that.

"Garnet?" Noah twisted on the chair, a compassionate look on his face. "I know that this seems odd to you, what I do. I try and hack into businesses to ensure that they are not hackable. If I can hack into them, then I work with that company to set up stronger firewalls on their sites. Now, your work site?" He waited for Garnet to nod. "It's fairly secure. There are some problems that need to be corrected. I have tightened up the security on your computer. Do you have a laptop?"

Garnet shook her head at that. She had never liked using a laptop.

"No, I don't. I prefer a proper computer rather than something that I can't work on." Garnet moved to stand closer to Noah. "What did you find?"

"What did I find? Who says that I found anything?" Noah grinned at her for a moment.

"You have to have found something. I can see it in your eyes." Garnet could hear Rowan's soft laughter as she said that.

"She's got you there, Noah." Rowan moved to stand behind him, a hand resting on his shoulder. "Tell us. What did you find?"

"Someone has tried hard to get onto your computer, Garnet. You have really good protection on it. I am working on tracking it back but it seems to go back to your company. How well do you know anyone who works there?"

Garnet stared at him in horror. She had not expected to hear this.

"Not well. I applied on line and was accepted that way. All my work is received and submitted that way." Garnet sighed. "I guess that I stop working for now."

"It would likely be better. Someone just might get through." Noah didn't say what all he thought. He didn't have to.

Gideon wrapped his arms tight around his lady. This is what he had expected to hear but hoped that he would not.

“Okay, then, Garnet. We’ll find something for you to do to fill in your days. For now, let your boss know that you’re taking a break. Have you finished everything that you were working on?”

“I have.” Garnet moved away from him in an abrupt manner, her thoughts in turmoil.

“Who is doing this, Noah? Who is after me that badly?”

Noah had been watching her closely. He had no idea who was after her but he was determined to do his part to find out.

“You’re a victim here, Garnet. Rowan deals with victims of domestic violence. She can give you good tips on how to stay safe. I hear that Abe, Don, and Richard are working on that as well.”

“They are. They want to wrap me in bubble wrap and stick me away somewhere. Only, that won’t solve this. How do we do that?” Garnet turned back to face the others. “How?”

“We’re working on that, love.” Gideon watched her closely, seeing how close to breaking that she was. “Unfortunately, it wakes time. For now, let’s set this aside and just enjoy a visit with friends.”

Chapter 26

That Saturday, Gideon reached for Garnet's hand after she had shut and locked her house door. He was heading for a wedding and had asked her to come with him. She had stared at him for a moment before nodding. She guessed that this would be her life if she did in fact marry Gideon. They were still talking that way but she felt too dangerous. Gideon had laughed at her, telling her that they could be dangerous together. After all, God was in control and knew exactly what they were facing.

Gideon tucked Garnet into his car before he stood for a moment, staring around. He could feel someone watching them but could see no one. His hand raised for a moment as Don drove by, intent on watching out for his pastor friend.

Late that afternoon, Garnet twisted restlessly on her seat. Gideon's arm rested along the back of her chair, bringing comfort to her. He watched her closely before he excused them and was on his feet, her hand in his.

"We can leave, love." Gideon directed her outside, a wave to the couples who had gathered outside the building.

"Are you sure?"

"I am. Let's head out and grab a coffee somewhere." Gideon pulled away from the parking lot, heading for a popular diner. He paused for a moment as he pulled into the lot before he parked and ran in to grab coffees for them both.

Back in the car, Gideon paused to sip at his coffee. He turned towards Garnet to find her watching him in return.

"Gideon, what are we to do?" Garnet's voice wobbled slightly.

"We marry, love. We marry. I can't protect you as I would want to if we're not together." He bit at his lip. "My parents will be home next week. Is that too soon?"

Garnet turned her face to stare out of the car. She was devastated that she didn't have anyone of her own to plan this with. She blinked back her tears. This was not how she expected to marry. In fact, Garnet had never expected to marry.

Gideon's arm was around her, pulling her into his hug.

"It's okay, love. I know that it's hurting you to be on your own. Mom will help as well the ladies in the family. If you want someone else to help you, just say so."

"It's okay, Gideon. I just am afraid for your family. I'm too dangerous to be around them and I don't understand why. Nothing that we have found explains it at all." She looked at him. "And what about the church board? Aren't they worried?"

"They are, love. They are but they are behind us in every way that they can be. Let's meet tomorrow with my family, if you like. They are expecting us to marry quickly." Gideon kissed her, his forehead resting against her. "I do love you so much."

That next afternoon, Gideon paused as he walked in his parents' back yard. They had unexpectedly shown up the night before and their family had just descended on them. Garrett and Emily had been surprised when he introduced Garnet as the love of his life but Emily had simply swept Garnet into a hug and then with an arm around her had headed for the back porch. The six younger ladies had simply taken over the kitchen, leaving the men to take over the office to work on the mystery surrounding Garnet.

Garrett studied his son before he approached him, an arm across his son's shoulders. When did he get so tall, Garrett wondered? He's ready to take that next step but is concerned about the consequences of the danger that surrounds them.

"Son? What are you thinking?" Garrett directed their steps to the back of the yard and the chairs that were there.

"I'm not sure, Dad. I am at a loss as to what to think other than that I love Garnet deeply and don't want to see her hurt."

"And both of you have been." Garrett was a retired pastor who spent time going out on short-term missions.

"We have been, Dad. It's hard not to know why or who. We're looking over our shoulders to try and see who is following us. I'm afraid that someone will go after my people." Gideon buried his face in his hands. He felt his father's hand on his back.

“These are all legitimate concerns, son. We’ll pray them through. I gather that your friends are working on this just as they did for everyone else.”

“They are, Dad. Even Abe and Richard are weighing in.” Gideon looked up, a determined cast to his face.

“I gathered that they would be. And James is working it as he can.” Garrett prayed for his son, having been burdened greatly for him without knowing why. “Garnet? Her family?”

“They were killed a number of years ago, Dad. She has no one. And that is stressing her out so much.”

“It would. Your mom will step in.” Garrett sat back, his eyes on his grandchildren who were playing in the yard. He was grateful for each one and that they got along. It was a blessing, he knew. “When are you planning to marry?”

“Next weekend. I would be honoured, Dad, if you would do the ceremony. I haven’t talked to Garnet yet and I need to.”

Garrett nodded. He knew just how tender a heart his middle child had. He had always been like that. And what he was going through was troubling to Garrett.

Garnet turned to Gideon late that afternoon. They were both in the rose garden at his parents, facing off with one another. Garnet didn’t want to talk and Gideon was determined that she would.

“Garnet? What’s wrong, love?” Gideon reached for her hands, finding hers cold.

“Gideon? What are we doing? We can’t marry!” Garnet was beginning to panic. All she wanted was her mom.

“Garnet? We don’t have to marry next weekend. It’s your decision. I love you and want to take care of you.” Gideon waited patiently for Garnet to respond. “I know that you want your mom. I wish I could bring her to you.”

Garnet began to weep, finding herself folded into Gideon’s arms, feeling loved and secure and safe.

Chapter 27

That evening, Garnet curled up in a wicker rocker on her front porch. Twilight was dropping down and she could hear the sounds of nature settling down for the night or awakening, depending on what critter it was. She studied the moon that was on the rise as well as the stars that were beginning their twinkling for the night. Garnet wrapped her hands around her mug of tea, not looking at the table beside her. She didn't want to see the piece of paper that lay on it. She had read it, fear growing within her at the threats. Someone had been close enough to Gideon and herself to know what their plans were. She was afraid for her knight and his family. She just could not understand it.

A picture had been taken of the paper and sent to James. James had responded quickly, asking if she was safe. She had responded that she was but that she was afraid. He has replied that of course, she was. Could she just leave the paper where it was until the morning?

Garnet had sighed at that. She wanted that warning gone that night except that was not happening. She moved the small decorative urn that she had on the table to rest on top of the paper. She would ignore it until the next day as best as she could. Garnet had read it, freezing at the venom that spewed from the page. She had no idea who wanted her to suffer and even die, as had been threatened in the note. And Gideon and his family had been threatened as well.

Rising at last, she headed into the house, locking the doors behind her and then systemically checking each door and window. As much as she wanted the windows open, she would not do that. She was too afraid to allow any opened window.

James stared down at the threat the next morning. He knew that Garnet stood nearby. He could feel the fear emanating from her and didn't like it. He also didn't like the tone of the note.

"Garnet? When was this left?" James eyed her as she hesitated to answer. "Garnet?"

"James? Who is doing this? I've found things rearranged outside. There were disturbances in the garden. I can't go on like this. When I'm around Gideon, I am so afraid for him." Garnet looked terrified, James decided.

James' hand was out to turn her back into the house. He knew that a crime scene tech would be there to do what they did best. In the meantime, he needed to calm Garnet down. He turned as he heard a car door. Good, he thought. Gideon is here and can help calm his lady.

Gideon almost ran towards Garnet, sensing that she had had something happen that she had not told him about. The mind games that were being played with her? They were starting to take their toll. Saturday could not come fast enough, he decided, when he could take her to his home and try and protect her there.

"James?" Gideon's voice held a question.

"Garnet found a threat on the front porch. She found it last night. And now we have to figure out who and why." James looked past Gideon to where the crime scene tech was pulling his kits from the van. "Go on in to your lady, Gideon. I'll be in shortly."

Gideon stared at the little table, stepping to where he could read the threat before he headed into the house. He found Garnet just inside the door, her arms wrapped around her abdomen, tears on her face. This was not her, he knew. She didn't cry but it had come to the point where she was.

"Love?" Gideon wrapped her into a tight hug, feeling the sobs as they shook his lady's body.

"Gideon? Who is doing this? And why? Who hates me that much?" Garnet leaned into him, taking from his strength.

"I don't know. Emma was working on that, I think. I thought that we would have heard from her."

"I did. I haven't had a chance to open the email as yet." She paced towards her office, thumping down into her chair and reaching to wake up her computer. "I have no idea what she'll have to say."

Gideon's hand reached to rest on one of hers, stopping her motions. He simply bowed his head and began to pray for his lady and himself and that there would be a swift resolution to their trouble. He begged God for that, his prayer sprinkled with verses about peace and protection.

Garnet's head had bowed as Gideon began to pray. She felt peace for a moment but doubted that it would last. She sighed to herself. She was looking on the negative and doubting. That was not how she had been raised. Circumstances had driven her to that. Garnet began to pray for forgiveness and then for what Gideon was praying for.

Gideon looked at Garnet as she hesitated to open the email and then reached for her hand once more.

"Emma will have looked into whatever it was that she needed to. She'll have proven everything that she has sent you. It's how she works."

Garnet nodded, hesitating to look at the email. A word caught her attention and then she was lost in the information that Emma had sent her. She sat back, not sure how to take in the written words.

Gideon was reading as well before he asked Garnet to print off the email. She shot him a look before she did so. He was on his feet to retrieve the copies and then was back in his seat, reaching for a pen and highlighter. He read in silence, hearing the faint sounds from outside of the house.

Garnet read through the papers, a frown on her face. She had no idea where Emma had found her information but she nodded. She had learned that family history from her parents. She frowned though as she continued to read. Garnet sat back, a faraway look on her face. What did this mean, then? Who was this person who Emma had named? She was not familiar with them.

"Did Emma send this to James?" Garnet's voice was almost inaudible.

"I would imagine that she has. She'll have found information that he may not have." Gideon bit at his lip. "Garnet? What are your thoughts?"

Garnet snorted, bringing a smile to his face. She turned and then rose, beginning to pace.

"I don't know what to think. Not any more. That name? I know the name. I just don't know why." Her face paled and she almost ran back to sit in front of her computer again. Her fingers flew as she searched the website of the company for whom she worked. She sat back, her face turning even paler. "He's the president of the company. Why me? What did I do to him?"

Sobs shook her body as Gideon gathered her close to his heart. His eyes were on James who hesitated in the doorway. Gideon nodded at the pile of paper before James reached for them.

Chapter 28

James found a seat, eying Garnet for a moment. He needed to speak with her but it didn't seem that would happen for a while. His eyes dropped to the paperwork as he began to read. He frowned for a moment, his eyes raising back to Garnet, to find her watching him from the safety of Gideon's arms.

"Garnet? Do you know this person?"

"Not personally. But he is the president of the company that I work for. What have I done?" Garnet buried her face in her hands, sobs shaking her body once more. She was tested and pushed beyond her limits.

"The president? How would he know you?" James walked away, his phone out to contact one of the other detectives. A short conversation followed before he tucked away his phone. This was making no sense whatsoever. He returned to sit and face Garnet's steady gaze.

"I have no idea, James. That's something that you need to ask him. As to why? I don't know that either." Garnet bit at her lip. "I don't know that he would. And if he did, I don't know him other than having heard his name."

Gideon leaned his head against Garnet's, his arms providing comfort to her. He waited for her to speak more but she didn't. He could see the puzzled look and frown on her face.

“What was the letter about, James?” Gideon finally broke his silence, not taking his gaze away from his beloved lady.

“The letter? A threat of sorts. Garnet was warned not to talk to us or she would be harmed. You and your family were not in this warning this time, Gideon. Makes me wonder why.” James watched the emotions that flickered across Garnet’s face. “Garnet?”

Garnet shook her head. She had no idea what was going on or why. That was James’ problem, she decided. She looked at her computer as an email notification sounded. Reaching for the computer mouse, she opened the email. Garnet scrambled from Gideon’s arms, almost running from the room.

Gideon was on his feet, a hand on the top of his head as he watched her go. His eyes found James who was also on his feet and headed for the computer. James dropped into the chair, reading the email before he was on his feet and heading for where he could hear Gideon’s quiet voice. He stood and watched as Garnet refused to move towards Gideon and simply moved away from him if he approached her. James frowned and then his face cleared. She was trying to protect herself and protect Gideon at the same time. This wouldn’t work, though. Gideon was not going to walk away from her.

Walking to open the front door as he heard the doorbell, James motioned Garrett and Emily into the house. He shook his head at the question on their faces.

"James?" Garrett shifted on his feet to stare past him. "What's going on?"

"That's what I'm trying to figure out. Garnet received an email and ran from the office. She's not letting Gideon near her." James peered at Emily. "Emily? I know that she's really missing her mom right now. Would you?"

Emily simply handed her purse and the dress bag that she was holding to her husband and walked rapidly towards the kitchen. She gave her son a hug before she was by him and gathering Garnet into a hug. Garnet jumped at that and then simply melted in her future mother-in-law's arms. Sobs shook her body, sobs for what she had lost and what she no longer had but also sobs of fear and worry. This was not her, Emily had decided. She did not cry like this but given what she was going through and feeling, it was no wonder that she was sobbing like this.

Gideon was at a loss and walked away from his mother and his lady love. Garrett was waiting for him, hugging his son as he used to do when Gideon was a small boy and had been distraught. Gideon fought back his own tears but was not quite successful in that.

James walked back to the office, reaching to print out the email. He was angry as he read it once more. Who was this person who had threatened Garnet in just a horrible manner? He glanced at the door and then forwarded the email to himself. He would then forward it to the crime scene techs. This was now evidence, he decided, and knew that he would have to speak with Garnet about it. Only, James didn't think that would be happening. Not any time soon. He left after a quiet word with Gideon.

Gideon stood and watched his mother and his lady love. Garnet had gained control of herself once more and had stepped away from Emily. He could tell that she felt ashamed of how she had broken down. Emily had simply reached for the kettle. In her mind, a cup of tea for each of them was desperately needed.

Gideon walked through Garnet's yard later, his father at his side. He was searching for anything that didn't belong there. Only he wasn't sure what belonged and what didn't belong. Garrett didn't say a word. There were no words that he could say that would help.

Emily had turned to Garnet at last, setting down her mug.

"Garnet? I know that you're rushing into this wedding. Have you thought about a dress?"

Garnet drew in a shuddering breath, her thoughts chaotic. She frowned before she was running for her bedroom and shoving aside clothes in her closet. Emily had followed, not sure what Garnet was up to. She had brought her own wedding dress, which her daughters had worn, just in case Garnet didn't have one.

Garnet drew in a breath of relief as she pulled out a dress bag. She opened it and pulled out a beautiful wedding dress, now turned ivory with age.

Emily approached, surprise in her voice as she exclaimed at the beauty of the dress.

“This was your mom’s.” It was not a question but a statement.

“It was. I never thought that I would ever get to wear it. I just wish she and Dad were here. It doesn’t seem right to be going ahead with a wedding without them.”

“They’re here with you, Garnet, and in wearing your dress, you are honouring them. Does it fit?”

Garnet shrugged. She knew that she was about her mother’s size. She had held on to that dress although she had let other sentimental items go. She drew in a deep quivering breath.

“I don’t know, Emily. I really don’t know.” Garnet’s hand brushed down the dress. “I guess that I need to try it on. Dad always said that Mom was my size when they married. It hurts not to have them here.”

Emily helped Garnet into the dress, drawing in her breath at the beauty of the younger woman. She prayed for her, begging God to end whatever Garnet and also Gideon was facing. She feared for her son and his lady.

Chapter 29

Garnet paced the downtown area the next day. She had abruptly resigned from her position, not confident that she was safe working for that company any more. She had not spoken with Gideon that morning, avoiding his phone call. Garnet was deeply afraid and that fear translated into worry for Gideon. She didn't want anything to happen to him and that was just what she feared would.

Turning as she heard a voice calling her name, Garnet waited for Gemma and Glynna almost running her way. She was not surprised when she was hugged. It seemed that she was now welcomed into a family of people who hugged.

"Garnet? Aren't you working today?" Glynna stood for a moment, an arm around the other lady.

"No. I quit. I can't work for that company any more. The president may be involved in what is going on." Garnet felt relief at saying that, noting that she felt freer and more like herself than she had since she started working for that company. "And do you know what? I'm glad. I need to find new work but Gideon and I are discussing what I want to do. It's been years since I've felt this free." She grinned at the two other ladies.

"Well, then, how about some lunch?" Gemma pointed down the street towards a diner. "I just know that we'll enjoy our meal together. You are just who Gideon needs, did you know that?"

"I am? I guess so. I just didn't expect to marry so quickly." Garnet's voice died away as she felt a hand on her arm and then a hand was slapped across her mouth. She began to struggle violently, trying desperately to free herself. She could hear similar activity from Gemma and Glynna.

Despite their struggles, the three ladies were forced into a nearby alleyway and then through a door and down into a basement. They were shoved forward in a violent manner into a room. The door swung shut in a hard manner before a lock was snapped shut. Garnet flew at the door, tugging at the knob and then pounding at it, her screams to let them out going unanswered although the man standing guard heard them. He grinned in an evil manner. He had no idea who had employed him but he was being paid well to do what he and the other men had just accomplished.

Glynna and Gemma were searching for a way out before Gemma pulled out her phone. She frowned at it. For some reason, there was no service.

"I can't call for help, ladies." Gemma frowned up at them. "They must be blocking us in some way."

"I'm sure that they are." Garnet spun to face them, leaning back against the door. "I'm sorry. It seems that you two are now involved in this adventure or whatever you want to call it."

"It's not your fault, Garnet." Glynna reached to hug her, finding Garnet hugging her back. "Now, how do we get out of here? And what can we use for weapons?"

Garnet looked around before she turned to the door. She nodded to herself. The hinges were on the inside.

"I need something flat and metal." She looked down as a pocket knife appeared in Gemma's hand. "Thank you. Now, I wonder what we can use for weapons."

Glynna had been searching, finding a rusty metal pipe. She hefted it in her hand and nodded, before tiptoeing over to the other two.

"This. I suspect that there is someone outside on guard. What is your plan?" She studied Garnet, seeing the determination on her face.

"If I can get the hinge pins out, then we can pull the door out. Or at least I hope that we can." She placed an ear against the wooden door, smiling as she heard the guard being called away. "He's left. Let's see what we can do."

The three ladies worked together, Garnet working to remove the pins from the hinges. They were able to pull the door inwards and then peeked around the door frame. They ran for the stairs to the back of the building and were out of it and running for the diner in just a short period of time. They slid into a booth, looking around to see if they had been followed. Shock was on their faces that they had been able to free themselves and escape.

Garnet accepted the menu from the server, her hands shaking as she did so. She was deeply afraid and not just for herself but also for Glynn and Gemma. Whoever was after her had just upped the danger for them all. They apparently didn't care who was with her. That almost drove her to her feet and running for her car to drive away from a town that was welcoming her and from Gideon, who loved her so deeply.

Gemma reached for Garnet's hands, her grasp warm and comforting. She shared a look with Glynna.

"You're scared, Garnet. We understand that. We know that Gideon is as well. Let us help you work on this. Kidnapping us involves us." She looked around as footsteps stopped beside her. She slid over to let Toryn sit beside her. "Toryn?"

Toryn stared at the three ladies, just waiting for one of them to speak. He had been in the downtown area when one of the street youths had approached him and explained what he had seen. Toryn had been quick to call for assistance, sending the officers to the building and then searching for the three ladies.

"Toryn?" Garnet's voice was low and broken. She was at her breaking point, she decided. Only God could and would provide the relief that she was seeking. She prayed that it would be soon.

"Garnet? What happened? I know that you three ladies were kidnapped. Talk to me." His notepad was out to take their statements.

"I don't know. We had met up down the street and were heading this way. Suddenly, I was grabbed by the arm and a hand was slapped across my mouth. That happened to Gemma and Glynna as well. We were dragged into that building. We got the hinge pins out and escaped. Where are those men?" Her voice wobbled for a moment with her fear.

“The men? They’re in jail right now. We’ll be working through who they are. Gemma? Glynna? Care to add anything?” Toryn eyed the two sisters.

“What she said. Only I don’t know how she knew to take out the pins.” Glynn frowned at Garnet.

Garnet gave a quick grin. She explained that her father had done repairs around the home and had welcomed her assistance when she asked to help. Removing and replacing doors was something that she had learned.

Toryn walked away at last, a hand waving at Ben, the diner owner. He knew that Ben would forward any information that he was told. He sighed to himself. It was time to call in one of the security teams during the day. He had officers volunteering their time as well. Gideon was their chaplain and treated each officer with compassion. He had shown how interested he was in their well being in all ways, not just a spiritual one.

Chapter 30

Gideon stared at Garnet in disbelief and then horror as she recounted the adventure that the three ladies had shared. He shook his head. Broad daylight and all didn't stop the men. How was Garnet to stay safe when she couldn't even walk down a street in the daylight?

"I'm okay, Gideon. God provided me with the knowledge of how to escape. I just worry about Gemma and Glynna." She walked into his hug.

"That explains the texts that I got from Aaron and Bryce, asking what was going on." Gideon's chin rested on the top of her head. He was deeply afraid but could only hand that fear over to God.

"They texted you? I wondered if they would." Garnet moved away from Gideon. "How do we do this, Gideon? I want this over. You and your family are at risk."

"They are but we understand that it is only temporary." Gideon watched her as she thought through what he had said.

"It is, isn't it?" Garnet's face lit up. "So how temporary can we make it?" She reached for his hand and pulled him with her to the office. "Let's see what Emma has sent. Can we meet with someone if she has sent something?"

Gideon nodded. Don had been in touch, asking to meet with the couple that night. Toryn had reached out to him. James was away on a well-earned vacation that week. For that week, their investigation was on the side burner, waiting for him to return.

"Don wants to meet with us tonight." Gideon glanced at his watch. "Before we look at the emails, Garnet, let's eat something and then spend time in prayer." He wrapped her tight to him as she nodded. "I know that neither of us feels like eating but if you have anything for sandwiches, that works."

"I have cold meat and there are some salads that I picked up. Will that do?" Garnet was still learning what Gideon liked to eat.

"It will."

An hour later, Gideon raised his head from his prayer, Garnet wrapped in his arms. He would be content to sit there forever, he decided, but his lady was restless. He rose, reaching for her hand and then heading for her office.

"Are you all set for Friday night?" Gideon was but he wasn't sure if Garnet was.

"I am. That's not that far away. It will be a bit of a bittersweet day, though, with my family not here."

"I know it will be. You are surrounded by family and friends who are praying for you. You are taking on a deep, heavy task, my love, becoming a preacher's wife. But God has prepared you for that. And don't worry if you're ever uncertain. I am at times as well." He hugged her tighter. "Now, you were going to look at some emails?"

"I was." Garnet was reluctant to move but sighed as she rose to her feet, heading for her office.

She heard the doorbell ring and saw Gideon head that way. Don had arrived as had Richard. She frowned for a moment before her attention was on her emails.

Sitting in her chair, Garnet read through the material that Emma had sent. Where was she finding it? Garnet couldn't understand that. She felt an arm around her and leaned into Gideon.

"What has Emma to say?" Gideon's voice startled her for a moment and brought her back to the room.

"I'm not sure what I'm ready. I've printed off copies for us all. That way we can mark it up. At times, it's easier to understand the printed word on a piece of paper." She looked up at Don as he laughed. "Don?"

"I've got them, Garnet. Let's go through them and see what Emma has to say. She'll have found out something that will help move the investigation along." Don sat back in a chair, his eyes on the couple across the desk from him. He prayed for them, knowing that only God could bring this adventure to an end. He had seen it too many times.

"Don? What does this mean?" Garnet looked up, a finger pointing to a paragraph.

"What does what mean?"

"On page eight. The third paragraph. What is she saying?" Garnet was puzzled at what Emma was stating.

Don read through the paragraph and then back through it. He looked thoughtfully at Garnet and then at Gideon. Gideon was nodding as he looked back at Don.

"She's found this information for you, Garnet. It pertains to your family, I think."

"It does. I don't know how she found that out. I never knew that Mom and Dad had been threatened when I was a baby. They never said. Who is this man that Emma has said did it?"

Don read back through the paperwork, frowning as he did so. This was not what he had expected to hear from Emma. But what did they do with this information? Emma was still tracking down the information and promised to be in touch soon.

"I'm not sure what to say, Garnet. She is working on it for you and will certainly keep you informed as she finds out the information. She'll also pass it on to James."

"I don't understand though why she just found this. Has he been stalking me all these years?" Garnet drew in a quavering breath. "How do I do this, Don?"

Richard shared a look with Don. They both nodded.

"We up the protection around you, Garnet and Gideon. One of our team is with you at all times. I have two ladies on my team, Silver and Naomi. They will be with you during the day. Toryn has let us know that there are officers who will be on guard over the night. Gideon, the same for you. Don's team and the two men on my team will alternate with watching both of you. Now, when is your wedding?" Richard eyed them carefully.

"Friday night. And it is open to whoever wants to come. I can't say no to the request from the board to open the ceremony itself up to my people." Gideon's hand went up in the air. "I know. I know. It's dangerous but it is what it is."

Garnet shifted to watch the two security team heads. She was frowning, still trying to understand what had happened in the past and how it was affecting her today. Garnet was not sure that it was. She felt that it was someone else and that someone had to be related to the work that she was doing.

Chapter 31

Friday morning found Gideon at the church, staring at the menacing message nailed to the church door. His hand raised to tear it down before it dropped back to his side. He sighed. This is not what he wanted to find that day. It was supposed to be a happy and wonderful and joy-filled day. This was not starting it off like that. Paul approached him, wondering why Gideon was just staring at the door.

Paul looked past him, reading the vile and violent nature of the note. A hand on his arm drew Gideon away from the front of the church and back to his truck. They were not allowing Gideon to drive himself at present, someone available to serve as his driver.

"Gideon?" Paul shook his shoulder slightly. "Gideon?"

Gideon shook his head, his shock at the message slowly fading.

"Paul? Who says that kind of stuff? Threatening me, my family, my lady, my friends? And in such a vile manner?" Gideon sighed as he slumped against Paul's truck. "I know. I know. It's sin, pure and plain sin. I'm praying for that person, that God will work in his life. It's what we are to do, isn't it? We're to pray for our enemies."

"It is and not many of us do that, do we?" Paul turned his phone over and over in his hand. He had called James, who had not been surprised to find out what had happened. He had promised to head that way, sending patrol officers and a crime scene team ahead of him. "How do you do it, Gideon? How do you stay so positive in times like this?"

"God. I spend a lot of time in prayer and meditation, Paul. I have to. It's part of my work as a pastor but it is more who I am and how I was raised."

"I get that, but it still has to be so hard. Now, where were you headed inside?"

"My office. I have work to do this morning, calls to make, letters to follow up on. Anna will be here shortly." Gideon mentioned the church secretary. "We need to head her off."

"Already done. Come on. The officers have searched at the back door. Let's get you inside and out of sight." Paul frowned. "Is there any way that someone could have entered the building?"

Gideon shook his head.

"The alarm would have gone off. Even if the power is out or the wires are cut, the alarm goes through. That's the way it is set up."

Paul nodded as with a hand on Gideon's arm he pulled him around the church and then waited as Gideon unlocked the door and deactivated the alarm. Paul's hand stopped him in his tracks as Mark and Caleb moved past him, searching the church and then returning to nod at Paul.

Gideon waited somewhat impatiently. He needed to be done by noon, he knew, and that was cutting it close for what he needed to do. He turned as he heard other footsteps and frowned at Paul Rogers.

"Paul?"

"I'm here to help where I can and where you will allow me. We'll get you out of here in plenty of time to find your lady and your family. All is ready for tonight?" Paul smiled with sympathy as Gideon's eyes closed for a moment in relief.

"The plans are ready. It's the unknown that is bothering me." Gideon frowned at Paul as he gave a soft laugh. "You're enjoying this."

Both the Pauls with him grinned before Gideon headed for his office. He sank into his chair, his head bowing for a moment before he began to pray over his work, something that he always did.

Gideon worked steadily with Paul's help to go through what was needed. He was under orders not to appear in the office the next week. His father had been asked to step in for him, to allow him at least a week with his new bride. Gideon was afraid to do just that. He just knew that something was about to happen.

James appeared mid-morning, standing in the hallway where he could monitor Gideon. He sighed to himself as well, not wanting to approach Gideon. He was unable to do that when Gideon looked up and then was on his feet and walking towards him.

"James? What can you tell me?" Gideon rubbed at his cheek, distraught but hiding it well.

"Not a lot, Gideon, other than you two need to be very careful. We're working on the letter. It's rather brutal." James had seen worse but not when it was directed at a friend.

"I know that I do. We're trying to take all the precautions that we can." Gideon glanced down at his watch. "I'm off shortly. What else do I need to know?"

Jame shrugged. He had given all the advice that he could give. He had plans in place for security for that night. Other than that, James had no words. He watched as Gideon turned back to the office and his interrupted conversation with the board chair.

Gideon paced his office early that evening. Nerves were getting the best of him. Garrett watched his son, his eyes raising to the other three sons. He nodded before he reached to draw Gideon into a hard hug, holding on for longer than he usually did. His father prayer sounded through the room. He had done the same with each of his sons.

"Ready, son?" Garrett kept an arm around Gideon's shoulders.

"I am, I think, Dad. It's just this uncertainty that is surrounding us." Gideon followed his father from the office, his brothers trailing them, and headed for the sanctuary. He turned as he heard the music start and saw Garnet walking towards him, not surprised to see Paul Rogers escorting her. It was what his friend did.

Garnet faced the wedding guests later that evening. She had been somewhat surprised to see the number who had attended the ceremony and then took part in the light meal that followed. Emily and her six daughters as she called them had arranged what they called a tea for them, served in the gym of the church.

Garnet had been grateful. She leaned back against Gideon and looked down at the engraved rose gold ring that was guarded by her engagement ring. She had never expected to marry but to marry as she had? It had to be God, she decided. Garnet was still extremely afraid and worried.

Gideon felt the tremble that lightly shook Garnet's body. He reached for her hand, walking among the friends who were there, accepting the hugs from them all. He led her to the door, nodding at Don and Richard who were waiting.

"We're ready to head out, Don. Take us home and then we're leaving town. You have where we are planning on going. We'll send a text once we reach there." Gideon had made arrangements for them to head for a friend's cabin nearby. Don and Richard had tried their best to convince him to head for a town but Gideon had shaken his head. He needed to find his peace in the wilderness and to spend that time with his bride.

Chapter 32

A week later, Garnet moved through Gideon's home, now hers. She had been glad to be home or her home as it was now. While she had appreciated the quiet of the forest, she had been on edge to some extent. Gideon had prayed for her whenever he had seen the fear flickering in her eyes. For that, she was grateful.

Gideon set his phone to one side. He had ignored it over the week, revelling in the freedom from being on call for everyone who needed him. He had needed the break. His time with Garnet had been sweet and to spend it with his beloved bride in God's wilderness had been just what he had needed. He felt recharged and ready to find out who was behind everything.

"Okay, love?" Gideon dropped a kiss on Garnet's cheek. With his sisters' help, she had moved her belongings into the house the week before. She still had to set them around but that would come.

"I think so." Garnet hugged him. "Did you hear from James?"

"I did. He wants to meet with us on Monday. Nothing urgent has changed or come up, he said. Emma sent a text. She's forwarding material to us on Monday for us to look through."

Garnet sighed. It was about what she had expected him to say. She rested her head against him, finding comfort in his hold.

"We need to solve this, Gideon. How do we do that?"

"We work it as I would when I write a sermon. We start with the basics and move on from there. I know that my family who is now yours and our friends will help. We can do that on Monday night, if you're up to it." He smiled as he watched her frown as she thought through his words.

"That works. You'll reach out to them?"

"I have already. Don sent a text, asking to meet. He's agreed to Monday night. Their wives will come as well. Toryn and Slaney are on board." Gideon felt Garnet stiffen.

"Garnet? What did you think of?"

Garnet shrugged.

"I don't know." She walked away from him to the outside, walking around the house and studying it. She took in the late summer flowers and shrubs and heard the call of nature around her. Turning as she heard motion near her, she frowned at Garrett and Emily as they both grinned at her.

"You're here?" She reached to hug the parents who had just welcomed her into their hearts.

"We are. Gideon let us know that you two were home. I hope that we are not intruding." Emily reached to hug her son.

"Not at all, Mom. I have some meat to grill. Dad?" Gideon looked at his father, sensing that Garrett wanted to speak with him on his own, something Garett would choose to do if it was necessary.

“We’ll look after the side dishes, then.” Garnet moved towards the house, frowning as she felt something off.

The next morning, on the Saturday, Garnet leafed through the mail, frowning at the plain white envelopes, eight in number. She grew deeply afraid and dropped the letters on the desk and almost ran to find Gideon. Gideon spun as he heard her running footsteps and caught her as she threw herself at him.

“Garnet? Love? What happened?” Gideon’s face darkened as he looked past her, searching for who it was that had threatened her.

Garnet clung to him, sobs wracking her body. She decided that she was crying too much but just could not help herself. She prayed that God was indeed collecting her tears.

“There’s no one. But there are letters in plain envelopes. Eight of them. Who is doing this?” Garnet sniffled as she tried to control her tears. She could feel the heat of the day as they stood in the middle of the backyard. She really didn’t want to enter the house again but she knew that Gideon would insist on it.

“Letters? Come on, love. Show me.” Gideon kept an arm around her as he gently nudged her towards the house.

“I don’t want to.” Garnet tried her best not to walk that way but Gideon’s arm kept her moving forward.

"Are you ready for church tomorrow?" Gideon grinned at her, trying to take her mind off the letters in the office.

"No, I'm not. I don't know how to act as a pastor's wife." Garnet gnawed at her lip. "How do I act?"

"Just be yourself." Gideon paused in the office doorway. "The letters?"

"On the desk." Garnet refused to move into the room.

Gideon walked forward, frowning. He moved the mail on the desk.

"Garnet? You dropped the letters on the desk?" He looked back at her, seeing the shock on her face.

"I did. I dropped them there before I ran to find you." Garnet's hands scrabbled quickly through the mail. "Where are they? There were eight of them!"

Gideon searched the room before he looked thoughtfully at the French doors that opened onto the front porch. He walked that way, finding the doors unlocked even though he knew that they had been locked earlier. He opened the door and walked outside, studying the area and trying to find the letters. Gideon had no doubt that there had been letters. Garnet was too terrified for there to have been nothing. He stepped back into the house, finding Garnet waiting for him.

Garnet threw herself at Gideon, feeling safe in his arms. Nothing could explain the appearance of the letters and then their disappearance. She knew that Gorrie who had been around and bringing in their mail would have alerted them to the letters and would have contacted James to come and retrieve them.

Gideon studied the room, feeling something off. He scooped Garnet into his arms and dropped her into a chair before he crouched beside her and reached for his phone, sending off a text message to both Don and James. They would appear, of that he had no doubt.

Chapter 33

Don and Caleb walked the yard, staying out of the way of the investigating officers. They had spoken with the couple before heading outside. Don knew that the other four team members were around. James was with the couple, he also understood. He sighed. This is not how it was to be today. Gideon and Garnet should not be under a threat at this time. They should be enjoying the start of their life as husband and wife and that was not happening. Don knew only too well how that was.

Joshua approached him, frowning at the back of the yard.

"There's something back there, Don. I'm not sure what to think." He pointed that way and the three men walked there.

Don stared down at the pile of letters before he turned to Joshua.

"Go and find James. We'll wait here just in case." Don didn't put into words his thoughts. The two other men shared his thoughts without speaking.

Caleb walked around the back of the yard, frowning. This was bizarre, he thought, before he turned to stare at the back of the house. He gave a yell and began to run forward, startling the officers near the house. They turned as he pointed towards the house and began to run that way as well.

Don didn't move but he could not believe his eyes as Caleb pulled the man from his hiding place. How had the officers missed him?

James shot out of the office and around the house, startled by the shouts. An officer moved to stand in front of the French doors, her back to the outside. She trusted the officers out there to investigate and then inform her of what they found. Her eyes were on Gideon and Garnet who had risen to their feet and stood with their arms wrapped around each other, startled expressions on their faces which turned to fear on Garnet's. That was to be expected, she knew.

James slowly approached the man who was now handcuffed, He frowned. He thought that he should know the man but wasn't clear as to why. He took the proffered identification before he glanced down at it. Surprise coloured his face before he stared at the man.

"What are you doing here and hiding in the bushes?" James' voice was harsh. He waited impatiently for the man to speak. When he didn't, he handed the officer back the identification and directed him to arrest the man for trespassing and take him to be booked.

Walking towards Don, James shook his head. This was not only disturbing but also not understandable. Don stared past him and then back at him.

"James?" Don's voice held a question.

"Don? How did Caleb see him?" James didn't answer the unspoken question at first.

Don shrugged. It was how observant they all were and they reacted without having to explain themselves. It was who they were as a security team. They trusted one another and didn't question each other, knowing that each one of the team was dedicated to protecting whoever it was that was in their care.

"It's how we work, James. I can't explain it." Don watched as Caleb approached. "Caleb?"

"I know that guy, Don. He works for that copywriting company. In fact, he's the president. What is he planning?"

"The president? Again?" Don paced away from them, rubbing at his temple. What was this man up to? And why Garnet? That was something that no one seemed to understand. Not yet, any way.

James walked back into the house, a thoughtful look on his face. He had no answers to give Gideon and Garnet as they faced him with questions on their faces.

"Garnet. The man outside? He was the president of the copywriter business. Why is he stalking you?"

Garnet stared at him in horror, her head shaking. She had no idea why the president would be chasing and stalking her.

"I have no idea, James. I never met him. I mean, I never met any of the employees. I was hired on line and worked on line, never going to the business. Why is he here?" Garnet shrank back against Gideon, afraid for herself and for her groom.

"We don't know. He's not talking. Let's see what we can find out." James left a short time later, more questions in his mind than had been answered.

That afternoon, only Caleb and Joshua were left. They paced the yard, carefully on alert. No one expected anyone to appear again but they were taking no chances. Officers would be on duty once evening came.

Garnet paced the house, not putting away any of her belongings as had been the plan. Gideon finally approached her, his arms sweeping her close. They just stood, clinging to one another. The man had not spoken at all, despite asking for his lawyer. His lawyer was not available that day and would not be available until Monday. He would remain locked away until then.

"I don't get it, Gideon. I really don't. Why me? What did I do to him?" Garnet almost wept as she asked her questions.

Gideon had no answers for her. All he could do was pray for his lady love and beg God to supply the answers and soon. His feeling was that they would soon be through their adventure. Only, he had no idea if they would survive or not. That frightened him greatly.

"I don't know, love. I really don't know." He had asked Emma to search deeper into this man. She was already doing that but finding roadblocks in her research.

"I want this over, Gideon. I can't live like this any more." Garnet leaned back to look up at him, not surprised when he kissed her. "How do we go on the offensive?"

"Good question. I'm off on Monday. We'll head for Riverville and Emma. Maybe she'll have some answers for us. I know that Abe's security team is working on this as well. So is Richard's team. They're not letting any little bit of information pass by them."

Garnet chewed at her lip, a new habit that she didn't realize that she had picked up. She finally nodded, not moving away from Gideon. She was suddenly deeply afraid for him.

"I don't get it. What did I do wrong in working for them?" Garnet frowned at Gideon as he shrugged. "That president is creepy. Who else has he done this to?"

Gideon stilled. Was Garnet correct? Had he done this before? He released her to reach for his phone, sending off a text message to James. He received an immediate response from James, asking him what he meant. Gideon responded with Garnet's words to which James simply said that he would look into it.

Chapter 34

A week had passed. Gideon was back into his work as a minister, finding himself tired by the end of the day. Something was weighing down his spirit and he knew exactly what it was. The mystery of who was after Garnet was driving what they both did during the day. Neither of them had come to an answer as to why or who nor had anyone else.

Garnet turned from the computer that afternoon. She was bored, she had to acknowledge to herself. She had been used to working all the day. This felt like an enforced holiday. Garnet was talking with Gideon about what she wanted to do but neither of them had come to any real conclusion as to what that would be.

Hearing the doorbell, Garnet headed for the front door. Standing back in the shadows, she stared at the man who stood there. She had no idea who he was and was not about to open the door. Hearing her phone chime, she headed for the kitchen where she had dropped it to the countertop. She frowned at the message from James. He had sent someone to speak with her and he should be at her door now. Would she answer it?

Garnet hesitated as she reached for the door, unlocking it and cracking it open slightly. She kept her toes braced against it, ready to slam it shut if she needed to.

"Can I help you?" Garnet shuddered at the squeak in her voice.

The man turned, a smile lighting up his face. He recognized Garnet from the description given to him.

"You can, if you're Garnet. I'm Frankie Brennan, a detective from Riverville. Emma knew that we were heading this way and asked if I could drop off some material." Frankie pointed back towards his car. "My wife, Deirdre, is waiting for me."

Garnet squinted past him and then was out of the house and headed for the car, greeting the lady who had exited it. They walked back towards the house, finding Frankie grinning at them.

"You both need to come in. Gideon will be home shortly." Garnet turned as she heard a car and then moved into Gideon's hug. "We have visitors from Riverville, Gideon. Frankie and Deirdre."

"Frankie? Deirdre? Welcome but what brings you here?" Gideon greeted them before pointing towards the house.

"Emma. I spoke with James and he sent me your way. She had information that she wanted you to have right away. We were heading this way any way. Here's what she was sending." Frankie held up a thick envelope.

"Come on in. We'll pray over it first." Gideon watched the ladies enter the house, a hand resting on Frankie's arm. "Frankie? What is really going on?"

"As I said, we were heading this way. Emma does this sometimes, if there is something that she really wants to get into a friend's hand right away. You know that I'm a police detective and have worked with James before. He has a copy of what I have here."

"I know what you do. I was just not expecting to be on the receiving end of your generosity. I also know what you and Deirdre went through. Is she still scary?" Gideon grinned as Frankie broke out into a laugh, causing Deirdre to laugh as well, causing Garnet to frown at all three.

"It's okay, Garnet." Frankie had a hard time controlling his laughter. "Deirdre and I had an adventure during which time I found out what talents she picked up on the mission field and how scary she is."

Deirdre swung an arm around Garnet in a hug, still laughing at her memories.

"I'm not that scary, Frankie. I think you're scarier after all your work on the streets."

Frankie continued to laugh as he dropped the folder on the table. Gideon, still grinning, had moved around the kitchen, finding coffee for them and then helping Garnet pull out the cold meal that she had prepared, just cold meat, sliced tomatoes and cucumbers, and salads. Seating themselves, he prayed for the meal and then for resolution of their mystery.

Once the meal had been cleared away, Gideon reached for Garnet's hand and bowed his head to pray for them all. He knew that both Frankie and Deirdre had had danger in their lives and that Frankie still faced danger daily. He also knew that it was coming to a close for himself and Garnet. He worried greatly that he would lose her and had to continually give that worry to God.

Looking up, Garnet reached out a finger to touch the folder. She gave a shudder of fear before Frankie slid it towards her. Emma had spoken to him about her findings, asking that he stay with Gideon and Garnet while they read through it and answer any questions that they might have. She also asked that he give James the copy that she was sending him.

Gideon reached for the folder, his eyes on Garnet. He was worried about her. He studied her pale face, the dark circles under her eyes, and the fatigue that she was trying hard to hide. Gideon knew that she was not sleeping well. Neither was he despite holding the love of his life in his arms all night. Both of them were restless.

Reading through the paperwork that Emma had provided, Garnet frowned as she rubbed a finger against her forehead. A headache was forming and that made it somewhat difficult to concentrate. She was not understanding what she was reading.

"I don't understand what she is saying, Frankie." Garnet looked up at that point. "Who is she referring to? The president of the company that I worked for?"

"No, not him. His brother. They are fraternal twins. The president is the man who was arrested in your garden. His brother has been living on the other side of the country but returned here to live just a year ago. He is involved in the company as well, behind the scenes."

"A twin? That's strange." Garnet read back through the paperwork, taking the highlighter that Gideon had retrieved. "I don't understand why me. Do you?"

Frankie was shaking his head. He had gone over the material with Emma, questioning her with that very phrase.

"No, I'm sorry, Garnet. I wish that I did understand why. That way, it could end for you. You have never met them?"

"Never. I have never seen either one of them." She drew in a quivering breath. Her face had paled even more. "They were both stalking me?"

"It would appear so. I know that you're from Alberta and that you have never traveled outside of the country. Correct?" Frankie had gone into detective mode.

"It's true. We always planned to travel the country as a family but never got the chance." Garnet was sober as she looked back at memories that hurt her so badly. "So, once more, why?"

"I don't know, Garnet. That is something that we're all working on. Yes, I am working on it as it seems to come back to Riverville as well. Another friend from Elmton, Bill Buckley, who is a police detective, is working it as well. It seems to tie all three of these towns together. And we are investigating these two men. It seems to be expanding as well as to others in that business."

"How?" Garnet waved her hands. "Never mind. I'm not sure that I want to know."

Gideon had been silent, his arm resting along the back of her chair. He shared a look with Deirdre, who turned her attention back to Garnet. She began to speak, telling her story, and then that of her cousin, Timothy. She also explained how God had led through it all, despite the fact that they almost died. She also told how she had lost her parents over it all as her parents had been behind what she had gone through. Their mission had been closed as it had been used for nefarious means.

Garnet didn't shift her glance from the other lady. It almost seemed as if she didn't blink. She drew in a deep breath at last, shifting on her chair to study Gideon.

"So, in all of that, God was in control. You have no doubt about that. He led you both on the path that He had predetermined that you would walk, correct?" At their nods, Garnet looked back at Gideon. "And that's how we are walking. We don't have to like it. We can try and run away. We can try and do it ourselves. But it comes back to God's sovereignty, to who He is. He loves us and wants only the best for us. Sometimes, His best involves danger and death. We have to prepare for that. That hurts, you know."

"It does, Garnet. But you are correct in what you say. He is in control. He also never leaves us or forsakes us. That is a promise that He never breaks. He also has sent the Holy Spirit to be our Comforter. He hears each prayer, each time we beg for answers, and He sees each tear that we shed."

Chapter 35

James looked up from the material that he was working through, a frown on his face. There was something off about the day and he didn't know what. On his feet, he headed for Toryn's office, needing to bounce an idea off of the police chief.

Toryn looked up as James tapped at his door, beckoning him in. He waited as James paced around the room before seating himself in front of Toryn.

"James? You're puzzled? I gather it's to do with one of your cases." Toryn looked at the door again and waved Lyle in. "Lyle's here."

James nodded, still somewhat lost in thought. He was puzzled by the twins in the mystery surrounding Gideon and Garnet.

"I'm at a loss, Toryn, Lyle. I have no idea which string to pull to unravel this mystery." James stared at the floor, waiting for them to speak.

"Go over with us what you have. We'll work it from there." Lyle reached for the pad of paper that Toryn was handing him, making his notes as he listened to James. His hand went up to stop James. "What you said about the brother? He moved back from across the country?"

"He did. I was surprised to find out that he had a twin. Nothing had shown up in our investigation and I would like to know why." James was angry at that.

“Who did that part of the investigation? You would not have missed it.” Toryn shared a look with Lyle when he heard the name. There had been concerns about that detective. Now, Lyle would have to deal with it.

James walked away at last. He was somewhat more settled in his thoughts. It always helped to speak with Lyle and Toryn. They had experience that he didn’t have. With Toryn and Slaney going through what they did, he could give advice from a victim’s point of view.

Heading for Ben’s diner, James paused as he stared into a book shop window. He entered the store, seeking out the owner. A few questions were asked and answered before James finished his stroll to the diner. Ben waved at him before he headed his way.

“James? You’re troubled.” Ben slid into the seat across from James.

“I am. It’s this trouble with Gideon and Garnet. I don’t see what the whole mystery is. I’ve gone over and over the information that I have. It’s not making any sense.”

Ben nodded. He knew Gideon well, having spent many hours just talking with him but also in prayer with his pastor. He had come to know Garnet to some extent when she frequented the diner.

“I see. Let me go over what you know.” Ben succinctly gave the information, surprising James. “That’s what you have. What you don’t have is a motive. Why is she being targeted? And through her, Gideon?”

James stared at him. That put a whole new perspective on the investigation.

"You're saying Gideon, not Garnet. That she's being used to get to Gideon?"

Ben shrugged as he thought through it all.

"No, I'm not saying that. I'm just talking aloud, I guess. Have you considered that?"

James nodded.

"I have to some extent but haven't really followed up on that. How do you do this, Ben? How do you come up with the suggestions that usually are true?"

Ben shrugged once more. He had always been able to do that. When he was young he had wanted that ability to disappear. Over the years and as he had matured, he had thanked God for that ability to sort out problems. Ben knew that the street people trusted him and one of them had come to him that morning as he arrived. They had spent some time speaking. The man walked away, leaving Ben thoughtful as he unlocked the door to the diner and went about his early morning tasks.

Sliding a folded piece of paper across the table, Ben stared at James for a moment before he was on his feet, a smile on his face as he walked through the diner, greeting friend and tourist the same way. James watched him, moving his arms for his meal to be set in front of him. He reached for the piece of paper and tucked it into a pocket. He would look at it later, he decided.

Back in the office, James pulled out the piece of paper and prayed before he unfolded it. He stared at the name, sudden fear wafting through him. He was seated and researching the name before he reached for his phone and sent off a text to Emma, asking for her help. She was quick to respond that she would look into the name as soon as she was able to that day.

James drove away from the office, heading for the church. He knew that Gideon would be there. He needed to speak with him. Standing for a moment and staring at the church, James was torn in how to approach Gideon. Gideon walked towards him and just stood beside him.

"James, what brings you here?"

James spoke, giving the name that Ben had passed on. Gideon stared at him, shock on his face. He had had his own run-ins with that man who was not a member of the church.

"I've had my issues with him over the years. He's my age and we were in school together. We only shared a class or two. He wasn't into sports. In fact, he missed a lot of school. I was surprised that he even graduated."

"He did? Okay. I need to look further into him. I just wanted to see what you could remember about him."

"He wasn't someone that I particularly took note of. There were always rumours about him. What they all were now, I couldn't tell you." Gideon walked away at last, heading for his car. He was due to visit a church member in the hospital before heading for home.

Garnet turned as she felt an arm around her. She had been unsettled all day. She reached to hug her groom, finding his arms tight around her. She felt the kiss on the top of her head and then heard the prayer for them that he whispered. Garnet knew that something had happened with Gideon that day. She also knew that he would take time later to speak with her.

Chapter 36

Garnet moved through her house the next morning. Gideon was on a conference call in the office and she didn't want to disturb him. This was how it was some days, he said. Some days, he worked from home. Other days, he worked at the church. And then there were days when he was on the run with visitations.

Turning as she heard his footsteps, Garnet handed him his mug of coffee before she walked back into the kitchen. Gideon sighed, knowing that he needed to talk with her but wasn't sure how to broach the subject.

"Gideon? Are you heading for the church?" Garnet didn't look at him. Instead, she waited for him to respond.

"Not today. I'm working from here. What are you up to today?" Gideon watched with compassion as Garnet struggled with her emotions.

"I don't know, Gideon. I am so used to working. What do I do with my days?"

"I can't answer that for you, love. You are looking for something else to do. Take your time to do that. Meanwhile, I understand that our friends's ladies have a Bible study that they would welcome you to join."

"I have been invited. It's tonight." Garnet turned back to him, a frown on her face.

"That works. I have the men's Bible study. I can drop you off and pick you up. For now, I need to get back to my work." He reached to kiss her, not wanting to walk away from her but knowing that he needed to.

Around noon, Garnet frowned as she heard a sound at the front door. There should be no one coming to see them, not that she was aware of. She moved that way, a scream torn from her as the front door flew open. She could hear Gideon's running footsteps as he moved rapidly her way.

Gideon slid to a stop, his hands raising into the air as he saw the guns pointed towards him. Garnet was shoved away from him, much to his distress. He was prevented from following her as a gun was shoved at his ribs.

Garnet struggled to release her arm from the tight and hard grasp that the man had on her. She was unable to do so as she was hauled into the kitchen and shoved against one of the cabinets. She could hear scuffling from the entryway and prayed for Gideon, that he would not be hurt.

Gideon was shoved forward violently, losing his footing and thudding to the floor in the hallway, just outside of the kitchen. He could faintly hear Garnet's screams as he fell, his vision darkening for a moment. Struggled to rise, he was unable to do so as a heavy weight rested across his lower back.

Garnet stared in horror at Gideon was prevented from rising. She was still struggling to release her wrist but the man had too deep a grip on it. Her horror deepened as she saw the gun pointing down at

Gideon's back. Not a word was said by the men. Garnet jumped as the gunshot sounded and blood began to flow from the wound in the back of Gideon's right shoulder.

Screaming his name, Garnet struggled even more to escape before she was hauled from the room. Her cries and screams to let her go and let her help Gideon were ignored. She was slammed to the ground in the backyard where she lay, almost knocked unconscious. Garnet struggled to regain her breath, not realizing that the men had disappeared.

Sitting up, Garnet stared around, uncertain as to why she was outside. She struggled to rise, her body hurting from the way that she was handled before she was running for the house. Inside, she searched for Gideon, dropping to her knees beside him. A tentative hand reached to touch the blood on his shoulder. Her body dropped across his uninjured side as sobs shook her body. Garnet was beyond what her physical strength and emotions could take. She shut down.

Three hours later, a tap came to their front door which swung open. Gorrie frowned. This was not normal for his brother. The door never opened like that. He stepped through, a frown on his face as he listened for any sound and heard nothing. He began to call for Gideon and then Garnet, not hearing them respond.

Stepping further into the house, Gorrie stopped in horror as he saw the couple on the floor. He sprang forward to land on his knees beside his brother. A shaking hand reached to check for a pulse. Finding one, Gorrie's head dropped for a moment before he reached for Garnet. She too was alive but she was unresponsive. His phone was out as he called for help and then called James.

James threw aside the paperwork in his hands and ran for his car. He sped towards Gideon's, his siren blaring and lights flashing. He screeched to a halt before he threw the car into park and sprang from it to run towards where Gorrie was standing outside.

"Gorrie?" James was shocked at the look on Gorrie's face. "Gorrie?"

"James?" Gorrie turned to look at him for a moment before his attention went back to the house. "Gideon's been shot. I couldn't get Garnet to respond to me. I have no idea when or who."

James' hand drew Gorrie away from the house and to a leaning position against his car. He nodded as an officer approached, speaking quietly with him before he moved back to lean against his car as well. He was at a loss to explain to Gorrie what was going on. There just were not enough answers as of yet.

"James? Any answers?" Gorrie's voice was hoarse from his emotions.

"Not yet. It will be a while. I'll make sure that you get to the hospital." James beckoned for an officer to stand with Gorrie before he walked away, heading for the house. He stepped inside, hearing the frantic activity as the teams of paramedics worked on the couple. "Ed? What's going on?"

Ed, the lead paramedic, swung around briefly, catching a glance with James before he was back and working on Gideon.

"Gideon's taken a shot to the right shoulder. Close range from the looks of it. It's been a couple or three hours, I would say." He nodded towards Garnet, who was lying on a stretcher being worked on. "She's not shot but she's not responding to us. There are bruises on her wrist. Someone had her in a strong grip." His attention went to his partner who had started the intravenous line and arranged the oxygen mask on Gideon. "Ready, Pat?"

"I am."

The two men rolled Gideon slightly to slide the backboard under him. Once that was in place, hands reached to help lift him and carry him out of the house to the waiting stretcher. Gorrie shoved away from the car and was at his brother's side, a hand reaching out to touch his ankle. James' hand kept him from crawling into the ambulance with Gideon. He stiffened at James' touch and then relaxed before nodding. He watched as the ambulances raced away.

"I need to call Mom and Dad." Gorrie's phone was out but he was unable to see it for his tears. He felt hands on his arms keeping him upright.

"I'll look after it, Gorrie. Go with Ed. He'll take you to the hospital. Let me have your keys and I'll have your car driven to your home." James knew that all of the family would appear at the hospital, other than the children. He reached to call Toryn and asked for Slaney's help. Toryn was shocked, to put it mildly, and then rose to head for Lyle's office.

Chapter 37

Gorrie paced restlessly in the waiting room. His whole family had arrived, including his parents. They were all waiting impatiently for any word from the treating physicians. Garrett was waiting for James, on his feet and approaching the detective as he entered the room.

"James? What can you tell us?" Garett knew that the six other men in his family were grouped behind him.

"Not a lot right now, unfortunately. I wish that I did understand what happened." He looked behind him. "The physicians will be out shortly, they said." James walked away, his shoulders slightly slumped in discouragement.

Garrett watched him walk away before he turned to the men. He could see Emily and the ladies standing behind the men. He had no words to say. He walked towards Emily and drew her into a hug. He felt the sobs shaking her body. None of their children had ever faced anything like this.

"Dad?" Gemma spoke for the group. "Any word?"

"Not yet. And James didn't say what happened other than what Gorrie had said." He searched for and found Gorrie standing close to him, a lost little boy look on his face. His arm came out to hug his oldest son.

The physician treating Garnet stood at her bedside, staring down at her. There was nothing physical that was causing her not to respond. He shook his head. He had seen something like that only once before. Garnet had given up, he decided. The only one who would be able to rouse her? Gideon and he was under treatment in another room and not conscious himself. He turned and headed for the charge nurse, asking if Garnet had any other family.

"Gideon's family is waiting out there. She has no family of her own from what James said." The charge nurse was on her feet. "I'll go find Emily and Garrett. They'll want to be with her for now."

"Go ahead. Let me know when they're with her and then I'll speak with them." He walked away, the emergency department much too busy for his liking.

Garrett reached for Emily's hand before they followed the charge nurse. He knew that his family was standing behind them, wanting to come with them but understanding that they could not. He had frowned for a moment when the nurse said that the physician treatment Garnet had asked for them.

James stood to one side, watching the family before his attention was drawn to the woman standing on the other side of the room. He frowned at the look of hate that was directed towards them before he nodded to an officer. The officer approached the woman and drew her from the waiting room and to his patrol vehicle. James' attention then went back to those in the waiting room. He walked towards Paul Rogers who was waiting to speak with him.

Don appeared with his team, certain that they would be needed. Galway had called him, almost too distraught to tell him what had happened. It was what he had feared most, he decided, that one of the couple would be killed. He had no idea as to what shape either one was in.

Garrett and Emily stood and watched Garnet as the physician spoke. He could not tell them if she was injured or not. She had not roused at all. In fact, he felt that she might not for a while. It appeared that she had given up. Emily shot him a look and then moved to reach for Garnet's hand, to grip it in a strong and warm grasp.

"How is she?" Garrett spoke for both himself and Emily.

"She's shut down, Garrett. I don't know why and how long it will last. The only one who can likely get through to her is Gideon."

"And Gideon is not available." Garrett turned as another physician entered. "George?"

"I was looking for you and Emily, Garrett. Do you have a moment? I don't want to tear you away from Garnet." George Blake was a friend from church and the on-call surgeon that day.

"We can." Garrett reached for Emily's hand, following George from the room. The physician walked back to stand at Garnet's beds, staring down at her.

"George?" Emily's voice was broken. The worry for her son was evident in the tone.

"Emily. Garrett. I need to talk to you about Gideon. I understand that I should be talking with Garnet but that is not possible at present. As you were likely told, he was shot in the right back in the shoulder area. That is good. If it had been the left side, we would not be having this conversation." He watched with compassion as Garrett and Emily hugged. "Now, this shooting did happen a few hours before they were found. The blood had congealed around the wound. We need to go in and clean up the area and repair any damage that is there." He went on to explain the procedure and then held out a clipboard that held the consents needed for the surgery.

Garrett reached for the pen, his eyes on his son. He didn't want to sign but he had no choice. Gideon needed the surgery and Garnet was in no condition to sign for it. He scrawled his signature before he walked back to stand by his son's bed. A hand rested on his son's head as he begged God for healing for Gideon. Emily wrapped an arm around her husband as they stood back for the nurses to move the stretcher from the room.

Facing his family, Garrett drew in a deep breath. Never had they ever faced anything like this as a group. He had no words to share his feelings. Each of his children came to hug him before they headed for the outdoors where they gathered in groups. Someone had brought in the children who needed to be with their parents. Each child asked about their beloved Uncle Gideon in their own way.

Three hours later, George stood beside Gideon's bed once more in the recovery room. Surgery had gone better than he had expected. Gideon should regain full use of his arm but it would take time and a lot of physiotherapy.

Garrett and Emily looked around from where they had seated themselves near the door to the operating room. Garrett was on his feet, unashamed that tears were on his cheeks as George approached them. Their eyes raised to the ceiling, Garrett and Emily praised God that Gideon was alive and would heal. They then turned their prayers to Garnet and her healing. Garnet had not roused from her stupor and not one medical personnel could tell them when it would happen.

Chapter 38

James sat across the table from the woman who had been arrested at the hospital. His eyes dropped to the file folder that was open in front of him. He knew who she was and who she was working for. He just didn't understand how she was involved in Gideon and Garnet's lives.

The woman began to shift restlessly on her chair. The public defender who had been called in to represent her stared between the woman and James. He waited for James to speak.

James began to speak, detailing all the crimes that she had been involved in that could be confirmed. He looked at her, seeing the defiance on her face. He continued to speak, papers slid across the table to the lawyer. The lawyer studied them, his face growing increasingly grim. He finally stood, excusing himself and stating that he could not represent her. The lawyer walked away, leaving James to gather up the papers and walk from the room. The woman was led away and locked up in a jail cell. It would be days before she would be released.

Garrett rubbed at his face, fatigue weighing him down. He had sent all of the family home, telling them to work out a schedule to come back to visit the couple. He himself was not leaving. The nursing staff had been watching him with compassion as he found a seat in the waiting room and sat, his paper cup of coffee on the table beside him. His head bent as he prayed for his son and his bride.

Paul Rogers sat beside Garrett, his presence acknowledged by the other man, without speaking. He knew that Garrett would speak when he was ready. They were old friends. He himself had been speaking with James and the detectives, trying to help where he could to solve the mystery.

Gideon moved restlessly on his bed in the early morning hours. He reached for his right shoulder, not sure why it was hurting as it was. His eyes opened and closed before he slept again. Hours later, he was awake again and on his feet. Galway watched him as he dressed.

"Where's Garnet?" Gideon turned as Galway didn't respond.

"She's here, Gideon. The only thing is? She's not rousing. We don't know what happened to you two. You can't tell us and Garnet is not awake to say anything." Galway's hand reached to stop his brother from running from the room. "Wait, Gid. She's not been responsive at all. We don't know why."

Gideon's steps slowed almost to a halt as he heard his brother's comments before he was out of the room and looking for his bride. A nurse frowned at him, not aware that he was allowed to be on his feet and dressed. Gideon frowned back and in a rough voice that told the story of what he had been through asked where Garnet was. He was away towards her before Galway could catch up. James approached him, a hand out to stop him but Gideon dodged it and disappeared into Garnet's room.

Galway snickered at the look on James' face.

"He's on a mission, James. There is nothing or no one who is keeping him away from Garnet." Galway paused at the doorway, not wanting to intrude on Gideon and Garnet. He watched his brother bending over the bed. He could only imagine how he would feel if that had been him.

"I can see that. I do need to speak with him before he says too much." James leaned against the wall, his eyes closing for a moment. He was exhausted. This with Gideon and Garnet was stretching him beyond what he could handle as a human.

Gideon heard the muttered conversation from the hallway but his attention was on his bride. His hand cupped her cheek even as tears tracked down his face. She didn't move, didn't turn into his touch as she would have done, and just didn't respond. He had no idea why. An arm across his shoulders caused him to jump before he heard his father praying for him.

"Dad?" Gideon didn't turn to his father, not taking his attention away from Garnet. He could hear the sounds of the hospital around him but that didn't matter to him. The only one who mattered was not responding.

"You're on your feet. Should you be?" Garrett felt the shrug from his son who was refusing to look at him. "Gideon? Son?"

"I'm okay, Dad. I need to be here." Gideon drew in a quivering breath. "She's not responding, Dad. What did they do to her?"

"We don't know, son. Until she speaks with James, we won't know." Garrett looked over his shoulder. "James is waiting for you. Go with him and then come back. He needs to talk with you and you need to talk with him." Garrett's arm nudged his son away from the bed and towards James.

James continued to frown at Gideon before he pointed to a quiet corner in the waiting room. It would do for now. His hand was out to help Gideon keep his balance before they sat.

"Gideon? Talk to me. Tell me what happened." James was as ready as he could be, pen poised over his notebook. He studied his friend, seeing the changes that had come over him. They were not changes that he wanted to see in him but they were inevitable.

"James, what did they do to Garnet?" Gideon looked up at his friend, terror and hurt in his eyes.

"We don't know, Gideon. She was found lying with you, actually partly on top of you. She has not responded to anyone since she was found. The surgeon thinks that it was at least three hours before Gorrie found you." James watched him closely.

Gideon's eyes slid closed as James said that. He could only imagine the fear that had overtaken her. It was no wonder that she was not responding to anyone.

"I don't remember much, James. I answered a tap at the door and four men burst in. I don't remember much about them. I was just too scared for Garnet. They forced me towards her and then I was on the floor. I couldn't get up. I could hear Garnet struggling near me but I don't know why. Then I felt the pain in my shoulder and nothing." Gideon twisted to stare towards the hallway. He didn't want to be sitting here talking with James or any other police officer. He wanted to be with Garnet and only with her.

James nodded. Gideon had confirmed their suspicions. He reached into his pocket and pulled out a photo, studying it before he handed it over to Gideon.

"Do you know this woman, Gideon?" James didn't say anything more than that.

"Who?" Gideon stared at the photo, not seeing it but seeing Garnet's white face. He blinked and his vision of Garnet faded. He frowned before he shook his head and handed the photo back to the investigator. "No, I can't say as I do. Why?"

"She was arrested on this floor last night. She was very interested in what was going on with you two. She's not talking and has refused to give her name. We are working on identifying her."

Gideon nodded once more before he was on his feet. He staggered for a moment to keep his balance, a hand out to brace his arm in the sling. His feet took him back towards his beloved lady, the door swinging shut behind him.

James stood and watched him, puzzlement on his face. There had to be something in what happened to explain it all. Only there didn't seem to be. He reached for his phone and read the text message before he was almost running for his car and heading for the crime scene tech who had an interesting object to show him.

Chapter 39

A day had passed since Gideon had regained his feet. He refused to go back to his room, insisting that he needed to be with Garnet. Nothing that the staff tried worked. George had finally shaken his head, moved in a recliner for Gideon, assessed him, and walked away. The younger man was hurting, George knew, and it was just not a physical hurt. His emotions were torn in many ways. God was working it out. George just wished that he would hurry up and bring the resolution that was needed.

Late that afternoon, Garnet's head began to toss. She was fighting the hands holding her, convinced that she was still a captive. Gideon's heart broke for his lady even as he gathered her as close to his heart as he could with one arm. He had reached for the sling, ready to toss it to one side but Gemma's fierce glare at him had stopped his hand. His words of love were whispered in Garnet's ear.

Garnet stopped moving, afraid to as she felt herself held. She heard the voice murmuring to her but was afraid that it was her captor. Her mind began to clear as she recognized Gideon's voice. Her eyes just refused to open as she slept, this time a sleep that was normal.

Gideon held her, his shoulder hurting even as he did so. He didn't want to let Garnet go, afraid that she would drop back into that well where there seemed to be no escape from. He felt hands on his arm, causing him to release his bride to her bed despite his protests. Galway and Gareth moved him back to his chair.

"She's sleeping, Gideon." Gareth had dropped by on his way home, praying that Garnet had roused and was talking. "She'll sleep. For now, you're coming with us. Gemma and Ginny are here and will come and find us. The nurse says that you have refused to eat. We're finding you something to eat and you will eat." Gareth was stern with his brother, knowing that he had to be.

Gideon moved away reluctantly after dropping a kiss on Garnet's cheek. He didn't want to be away from her, afraid that something would happen to her while she was not in his sight.

'Stop doing God's work for Him, Gid." Gareth swung an arm across his brother's shoulders. "He is in control of this."

"I know You're throwing my words back at me." Gideon grinned for a moment. "I tend to do that. I have to release Garnet. Only it hurts to do so."

"We get that. We've all had to do that at some point but not to the extent that you have." Galway carried the tray with their food towards an isolated table. He wanted to talk with Gideon but he didn't want anyone to overhear them. "This table should work."

Gideon sat slowly, exhausted beyond what he had ever experienced. He knew that he shouldn't be up but he had to be. God understood, he knew, but he wasn't sure if the humans around him did.

The couple sitting near to the three men kept their eyes on the three men. Galway frowned at them before he reached for his phone and snapped a few photos of them that he forwarded to James. Hopefully they were innocent but it didn't appear that they were. He was deeply worried about his brother and his wife. This was uncharted territory for them and only God knew how and when it would end.

"Gideon? What happened yesterday?" Gareth bit into his sandwich as he waited for his brother to speak.

Gideon shrugged. He had no idea what had really happened.

"I don't know, Gareth." He recounted what he could remember. "I don't know what happened to Garnet. I think the physician is correct. She has shut down. How do we get her back?" His hand went up as Gareth's mouth opened. "I know. It's in God's hands. This is hard, you know? I know that I usually am the ones saying the words. It's different when it's you. It's hard to trust and belief and keep hands off."

"It is. But it will help you as you work with other victims." Galway nodded at Gideon. "That's what you are, Gideon. A victim of crime as is Garnet. Neither one of you will ever go back to where and who you were. But God will use this to work though you. You know that better than we do."

"I know, Galway. It's just so hard to be the one going through this." Gideon stared at the couple, not really seeing them. He dropped his half-eaten sandwich back on his tray. He was hurting physically but emotionally he was in rough shape. “I need to find Garnet.”

Galway walked off with his brother, leaving Gareth to clean up their mess from the table. Gareth watched as the couple too rose and followed his brothers. A frown covered his face as he followed them, feeling like he was playing detective and not wanting to do that.

Gideon paused as he saw his father walking towards him. He felt like a little boy who had been hurt without knowing what the reason was. He walked into his father's hug, finding his father holding on tighter and longer than he usually did. This was how his father was, he knew.

"Okay, son?" Garrett studied his son, seeing the changes in his son that he didn't like. He had to leave that with God, he knew. And that was difficult to do. As a father, he wanted to make it all better for Gideon and couldn't.

"I don't know any more, Dad." Gideon bit at his lip, hesitating before he questioned his father. "Do you see that couple behind me? Do you know them? They seem to be following us."

Garrett shifted on his feet so that he could study the couple. He sighed. He knew them. Garrett had had difficulties with them in the past when he had worked for the mission in town.

"I know them, son. I have had dealings with them. They tried to close the mission but were unsuccessful."

"I see. Then why me? What have I done? I am not part of that mission family, not really." Gideon was puzzled at that.

"No, you're not but because you are a minister, my son, and somewhat connected to the mission as part of your work, you are a target of them. And there is James and some officers."

The two men watched as the couple were led away despite their protests. Gideon sighed. He just wanted to sleep, the pain from his wound growing each moment, but he wanted more than that for Garnet to awaken and be herself. He walked that way, staggering somewhat as he did so. His father and brothers watched him, wanting to reach out and help him but knowing that he had to do this on his own. It was how life worked.

Chapter 40

Garnet's eyes flickered open late that night. She could feel the terror rising in her as she searched the room. A hospital room? How and why? Garnet felt an arm around her and stiffened. Who was that? She cautiously turned her head and frowned at the man who lay on the bed beside her. Who was he? Then, memory returned. It was Gideon. Only he shouldn't be here. He had been shot and she had been convinced that he was dead. God must have intervened. Her hand raised to touch his face, causing him to shift in his sleep.

Looking around, Garnet studied the intravenous line that ran to her hand. Hearing footsteps, she jumped before looking at the nurse. The nurse, surprised to see Garnet awake, smiled at her before moving quietly around the bed.

"Garnet? Can I get you anything?" The nurse waited for Garnet to respond, surprised when she didn't. "Garnet? Here. Let me get you some juice or ginger ale." She was away and back with orange juice and ginger ale. She waited for Garnet to respond, frowning when Garnet didn't, just smiling.

Garnet could not speak. She was afraid to. The man who had carried her from her home had threatened to come back and kill Gideon's family if she did speak. She had thought that Gideon was dead. Her fear had driven that ability from her. She turned to face Gideon once more, drifting off to sleep.

The nurse stood just outside of the hospital room, staring in at Garnet. There was something wrong, she decided. There was no reason why Garnet could not speak. It was as if the ability to do so had been torn from her. She shrugged and headed for the nurse's station to make her notes. She knew that the physician would assess Garnet in the morning.

The physician stared at Garnet early the next morning. He was just beginning his hospital rounds and had not expected to meet opposition from Garnet. He could not explain to Gideon why she was not speaking. Gideon had been distraught at the news.

"I'm taking her home, doc. She doesn't need to be here." Gideon turned as a nurse approached. "I'll wait outside." He walked away, finding James standing and waiting for him. "James?"

"Heading home, Gideon? How is Garnet?" James frowned at the look that crossed Gideon's face. "Gideon?"

"She's refusing to talk, James. Nothing I say to her makes her respond verbally. What did they do to her?"

James was nodding. He had seen that before when the fear had driven a victim to speechlessness. He searched for someone who could understand and nodded. He knew of at least two couples, one the police chief and his wife from Elmton and the other the minister and his wife from the same town.

"I know of two couples that this happened to. I'll put you in touch with them. In fact, you likely know Silas and Madigan."

Gideon nodded, his mind not quite on what James was saying.

"I do know them and had forgotten their story. I'll reach out to them." Gideon reached for Garnet's hand with his free hand. She was refusing a wheelchair, despite the nurse's protest.

James took the paperwork and walked away with the couple, his eyes searching the people walking around them. Something was off that morning, and he just couldn't not figure out what it was.

Gideon walked back towards the kitchen. Garnet still refused to talk to him, her eyes pleading for understanding even as she hugged him and then turned away. His shoulder was aching and he needed to sleep but he refused to do that. He had to be alert for Garnet and protect her. Just how that would be possible, though, Gideon did not know. He was not a fighter, not in a physical sense. He stood at the counter as he waited for the coffee to perk, smelling the aroma of the soup that his mother had left that morning in a crock pot plugged into an outlet. He appreciated that.

Garnet stood for a moment, her hair still wet from her shower. She had changed her clothes but still felt grubby. She didn't understand why. Walking towards Gideon, she moved into his hug, sobs shaking of their bodies.

Their meal over, Gideon reached for Garnet's hand as his head bowed. He was too strong of a believer not to trust God with their lives and with what they had been going through. So far, it was nothing like some of his friends had faced but they had still faced danger without knowing why or who. That disturbed and troubled him.

His prayer finished, Gideon reached for the pad of paper and pen that sat nearby. He shoved them across to Garnet, who frowned at him.

"We need to talk, Garnet. Only, your voice is locked inside of you." Gideon reached to kiss her. "We'll work through it but first, write down what happened. I don't remember much."

Garnet nodded, her head bending as she did just that. She didn't rouse from her work as Gideon stood and walked to the front door, opening it to find both James and Toryn there. He beckoned them in and pointed to the kitchen.

Finding seats, the three men conversed quietly as Garnet wrote away. She looked up at last, fatigue on her face, as she shoved the papers towards James. He needed them but she also wanted Gideon to know what happened. James shifted the papers so that both men could read before he handed them over to Toryn.

"Garnet? You don't remember what the men looked like? They said nothing?" James had been afraid that this was what would be told to him. "It's okay. You've done well. We'll work with what we have. But in the meantime, we need to keep you both safe. How do we do that? Gideon will be back at work and out in the community. So will you, out in the community, I mean. We have officers volunteering to be with you both. And Don and Richard are on board."

Leaving after an hour, Toryn paused to look back at the house. He had a bad feeling about the next few days as did James. They spoke quietly before moving to their vehicles. Toryn did not drive away right then. He watched the traffic moving along the street, alert for anything that seemed out of the ordinary. A passing car caught his attention and he pulled out to follow it. He sighed to himself. This was similar to what he had gone through with Slaney. It was not easy at all to continue to live life while being under an unknown threat.

Chapter 41

Three days later, Garnet raced for her home, slamming the door behind her and locking it. She sank to the floor, her back to the door. She could hear the hammering against it and the hoarse and coarse yells from the two men. Garnet's head was buried in the arms folded on her knees. She was too scared to even reach for her phone or pray.

James and his fellow officers ran for the front of the house. He had received word from Ben that someone was on his way to Garnet's home with the intent purpose of abducting her. The men were quickly subdued, handcuffed, and shoved into patrol vehicles. James knocked at the door, calling for Garnet, but getting no response. He turned as he heard a voice.

"Emily? You're here? Can you get into the house?" James pointed at the door.

"I can. Let me go in the back door though." Emily almost ran around the house, James keeping pace with her. Unlocking the door, she entered, James at her heels. She searched, finding Garnet still huddled against the door. She dropped down beside her, not touching the younger lady. She began to hum and sing her favourite hymns and choruses.

Garnet felt her body relaxing as she listened to the promises. She leaned against Emily, sensing the mother love from that lady. Her head raised as she startd at James, who had dropped to the floor as well. He was content to wait for whatever response Garnet could or would give. He heard footsteps behind him and then Gideon was past him to gather Garnet to him as best as he could.

"Having an adventure without me, love?" Gideon could not wait for Garnet to speak. He wanted answers and wanted them right away.

"I am." Garnet's voice sounded hoarse and rusty but at least she was speaking. "Those men? They meant me harm." She scowled at James as he grinned at her. "It's not funny, James. Who are these men? You arrest some and more appear. How many are there?"

"I agree with you that there have been a lot. We have narrowed down the group to one business. We still have some information to find on the owner of that business, but he knows you, Garnet. He has ties to your hometown." James said some names, causing Garnet's face to pale even more before she buried it against Gideon. "Gideon, you know them as well."

"I do. This is our connection, isn't it? And how is he connected to the copywriting service that Garnet worked for?" Gideon went straight to the centre of the problem.

"He's connected. A silent partner from what we understand. We need you two to be very careful for the next few days. We are almost at the point where we can arrest them, but we need you to stay as safe as you can."

"We know that, James. It's not going to be easy though. We have that conference starting Thursday night at the church which runs until Sunday. We have to be there." Gideon rubbed at his forehead with his left forefinger. A headache was beginning and that bothered him. He didn't need it at that time. He sighed to himself even as his arm tightened around his bride. He could feel the fear running through her body.

"We'll make sure that we have security around there. Don already approached me about it. He's calling in both Richard and Abe and their teams. His team will concentrate on you two. The other two teams will mingle among the participants and we will have officers there as well. We'll do what we can to keep you safe."

Gideon nodded, not fully concentrating on what James was saying. That was not his area of expertise and therefore he didn't take in the full ramifications of what needed to be done.

Thursday night found Garnet troubled. This was the first big test of her as a pastor's wife and she just didn't think that she could do it. She turned as Gideon hugged her, hugging him back.

"I don't know about this, Gideon. I'm not a pastor's wife. At least, I don't think I have that capability." Garnet was extremely sober as she spoke.

"You are the pastor's wife that I need and that our church needs. God knew that you would be my bride and the pastor's wife. He is walking beside us and has gone before us. Let's pray before we head out into the fray as is said." He kissed her before bowing his head. He knew that only God was standing between them and danger.

The three security teams moved among the participants, alert to any danger. They could feel it, their training kicking in. They just didn't know who to watch for and that made it much more difficult and dangerous to protect the couple.

Sunday morning found Gideon on his knees at his home office chair. He had risen hours before to find his prayer corner and spent that time just waiting for God. He didn't need to pray He knew that the Holy Spirit would pray for him.

Garnet crept quietly through the house before she found Gideon and then was on her knees beside him, his arm catching her close to him. She shuddered in fear for a moment, somehow sensing that today would be the day that completed the path that they were walking in this danger that they fought against.

Early that afternoon, Gideon stood in the sanctuary. He was exhausted, as he always was after such a conference. He was glad that there was no evening service. He didn't have the strength to go through another meeting. Footsteps stopped beside him as Don came to a halt.

"All set, Gideon?" Don was not rushing Gideon. He simply needed to know if they were ready to head out.

"I think so." Gideon squinted at Don. "Where's Garnet?"

"In your office. Paul moved her there once the service was over. He can keep a better handle oh her safety there. My team is moving through the church as is Richard's. Abe's team is outside."

"I can't thank you enough, Don. You have been a good friend over the years. Who would have thought when we were friends in youth group and high school that we would both face danger as we did?"

Don nodded, his own thoughts running along the same lines. Hearing a slight sound, he turned before his hands went into the air. Gideon stared at him before he too turned. His own hand was raised.

The four men stood in front of them, not moving and not saying anything. They didn't need to. The evilness of their nature was etched on their faces. Don glimpsed movement at the door and kept himself from nodding. Mark had peeked around the door and then disappeared. He would ensure that Garnet got out of the church safely and was kept that way. Don had no doubt that James and his fellow officers had been alerted and were moving in.

Garnet looked up as Paul reached for her hand, pulling her out of the office. A finger to his lips kept her silent as they ran from the church and outside. Garnet was stuffed into a vehicle and the vehicle drove far enough away to keep her safe. She frowned as Paul opened her door and then just stood.

"Paul?" Her face paled as she saw the grimness of his face. "Gideon?"

"He's safe so far. Don's with him and the SWAT team is suiting up to move in." Paul didn't have to say anything more. He knew that Garnet understood the gravity of the situation

Chapter 42

Gideon's fear abated at he felt God's hand at work in his heart. He knew that Don was tense and alert but would make no move until and unless he had to. Gideon stared at the men and then recognized the man standing behind them. He nodded.

"Burton Cole. Of course, it's you. You've always wanted to take this church down. Just why that is? I don't know." Gideon shifted on his feet, moving slightly backwards, knowing that Don would do the same.

Cole sneered at Gideon. He had wanted vengeance for years on Garrett but had not been able to wreak that havoc. Instead, he had turned his attention to Gideon. Garnet? He had been after her as well, just because she was too well thought of for her work. She surpassed any of the copywriters that he had ordered his brother to hire. His brother, Carl, had hired her and refused to fire her.

"It's your father's fault. All he had to do was relinquish the reins of the mission. I wanted it. It would have been a perfect cover for my businesses." Cole was deep into crime in their town. He had just kept himself and his businesses on the right side of the law and barely. There had always been rumours about him but no one would come forward. They had seen the people die who had threatened to. Cole was ruthless in taking out anyone who stood up to him.

"Dad? No, I don't think so. The mission board stood against you. More importantly, God stood against you. You can't win against Him." Gideon shuffled backwards another step, praying that no one would notice. Don moved with him, knowing that each step could very well be their last. "But I don't understand Garnet. What did you have against her? And I know that you have kept track of her over the years."

"The copywriting. She was too honest." Cole paused, not wanting to give away all of his secrets. He didn't know that the SWAT team was standing behind him with James standing with him, his phone out to record the conversation taking place. "The ones who I hired? They were working instructions into their copywriting. We couldn't get Garnet to do that. For some reason, she wasn't following instructions."

"God. He kept her from doing that. She was protected from being charged as an accessory." Gideon's voice was confident on that. "But what instructions were you having them write? Tell me. I'm very curious about that."

"Instructions? Sure, I'll tell you. The instructions were being sent out over our network to our people all over. They followed them exactly as they were told to. Garnet? She just didn't get what she was supposed to include. When she was ever questioned, she just said that she didn't have the set of instructions that the others had. We knew that she did."

Gideon gave a grim smile. Of course, he would say that, and of course, Garnet would say that. She never had the instructions. He frowned at Don for a moment.

"You reach out to Garnet's hometown, don't you? And I would suspect that you had something to do with her family's deaths." Gideon was grasping at straws at this. That was, until he saw the anger and evil that crossed Burton's face. "Of course, you did that. You drove her from her hometown and this way. You wanted to control her and keep her under your thumb. Only it didn't work out that way. She walked away from you."

"She did and she will pay for it. Where is she?" Burton moved towards Gideon, stopping abruptly as if he had run into a wall.

"I have no idea but I would imagine that she is somewhere safe. Our friends have taken care of that." Gideon stepped back once more, confidence in his bearing. James and Don exchanged a look. This was different from Gideon. He was always confident but this was something that had not expected. "You won't escape, Burton. Not this time." Gideon threw himself sideways as weapons were raised and pointed at him. Don threw himself the other way before he belly crawled over to Gideon and with a hand on his back, kept him on the floor.

The SWAT team moved in quickly, the men's weapons torn from their grasp before handcuffs were clicked around their wrists. Burton's minions did not struggle, knowing full well that the gig was up. Burton, however, struggled to escape, loudly proclaiming that he had done nothing wrong and that he was being falsely arrested. James stared at him in disgust before he walked past him to where Gideon was now on his feet, Don and some of his team surrounding him.

"Gideon? You okay?"

Gideon nodded, his only thought on his bride.

"Garnet?"

"She's safe. Paul pulled her from the office when he realized what was going down. They moved her away from her. Not that far, Gideon." Don knew that it would be a while before Gideon would be free to leave. It was the same for him.

An hour later, Garnet looked up as she sensed Paul moving. He had stood motionless for the last two hours, she decided, not sure if that was correct or not. He turned to her with a grin. Before he could say anything, Garnet had simply jumped from the truck, searching for her groom. Seeing Gideon walking towards her, she raced towards him, flinging herself at him. Gideon caught her in one arm, grimacing as he did so. As he had walked towards her, his left hand had supported his right arm. When he had thrown himself to the floor, despite his best efforts he had jarred his right side, driving pain through the wound and his body. Adrenalin had kept him from feeling pain until now.

Garnet and Gideon were escorted at last to their home, Don walking through their house before he nodded at them and left. Gideon stared at Garnet for a moment before he wrapped her into his arms and both wept. Gideon's voice began to raise towards heaven that God had protected them and brought them through everything. Garnet leaned harder against him. She was almost asleep on her feet. The release from danger had sent fatigue wafting through her body.

Gideon felt her slumping against him. With an arm around her, he turned her towards the bedroom. Afternoon or not, they both needed to sleep. His phone hit the night stand before he drew a blanket over them. They slept, not hearing the chiming of their phones. They would gather with their families later that week to just hear the confirmation of why Burton had been after them. It was just as he had confessed to Gideon.

Epilogue

A year later, Garrett studied the backyard of his home. It was full of his family. He smiled. Today had been a great day. Emily hugged him on the way by before she turned to the little ones who were clambering for her attention.

Garrett turned his attention to his children, all seven of them. Gorrie and Belle with two children. Ginny and Paul with two girls and a baby boy, Galway and Brenna with two young girls, Gemma and Aaron expecting their first, a girl soon to arrive. Gareth and Annie with their son Andrew, and Glynna and Bryce with two sets of twins, two girls and then two boys. His attention turned to his middle child, Gideon. He had feared greatly for Gideon and his bride, Garnet, as they had gone through their adventure. Garrett smiled as he watched them.

Gideon stood with his arms around Garnet, hugging her tight to him. They had grown in their faith through what they had gone through and their love had as well. Garnet had shared with Gideon that they too would be expanding their family but they had decided to wait to share the news. Today had been about celebrating their family.

Garnet shifted on her feet. She had been taken in as a member of Gideon's family. No one had blamed her for bringing danger to the family. It was not her fault, they had all told her in their own unique way. She had become a beloved aunt to the children.

Gideon cleared his throat, unsure how to broach what he wanted to say.

"Are you okay, Garnet?"

"I am, Gideon. Just as you are. Thank you for being who you are." Garnet reached to kiss his cheek. "God prepared us for each other." Garnet's gaze drifted among the family, stopping as she watched Garrett cuddle the youngest grandchild. Her gaze lifted for a moment and she frowned before her face lit up. "Mom! Dad! Daniel!"

Gideon stared at her and then followed the track of her gaze. He could see no one other than his own parents.

"Garnet?"

Gideon's voice caused Garnet to blink. When she opened her eyes, the vision was gone.

"My family was standing behind your parents, Gideon. They looked well and happy. But it wasn't true." Garnet sobered, wiping at a tear. "I miss them so much. I want them here to share our life."

"And they are. We just can't see them." Gideon looked back towards his parents and then down at Garnet. "You know, sometimes God lets our families return to earth for just a moment, just to let you know that you are loved and that they are okay. We'll see them again but sometimes we need that little bit of a God moment to help us."

Garnet was nodding. Her father had often spoken of that. She just didn't expect it to be given to her.

“I know, Gideon. I know. I can walk forward now, knowing that they are safe. I mean, I always knew that but I just missed them so much. They were torn away from me in such a had manner. I’m glad that it was not murder that took them.”

Gideon wrapped her tighter in his arms. His actions had always told her that he loved her as did hers.

“I love you, Garnet. I have since I think I first laid eyes on you. I never thought that we would marry. I don’t want to lose you and that was what I was so afraid that I would.”

“I love you, too, Gideon. God was gracious. He protected us and brought us through this time of trouble. I look forward to walking through our life hand in hand and with the little one on the way, we will grow closer to God and to each other.”

“Well said, my love.” Gideon kissed her again, not seeing the smiles sent their way. His family loved Garnet as if she was a sister to them, which in fact she was. Gideon had needed someone special to fill his life and Garnet was just the perfect one for him.

Dear Readers:

Thank you for choosing the story of Gideon and Garnet. He has been vocal in wanting his story told and he finally got it.

God protected them both through the danger that they faced. Through it, He led them to a deeper realization of His grace, love, and protection. We try our best to live our lives without His guidance but it doesn't work out so well. No matter what we face, we have the confidence that He is beside us, will never leave us, and has gone before us.

As to the characters who show up, as always? Frankie and Deirdre's story is *The Storm*, book one of the *Haven of Rest* series. Don and his team are *His Defenders*. Richard and his team are *His Protectors*. Abe and his team are in *His Guardians*. Silas and Madigan are in *Strong Courage*. Toryn and Slaney are in *Toryn*. And Andrew and Phoebe are in *The Potter's Hands*. They love to walk into stories and help out. Noah and Rowan are part of *His Warriors*. Timothy and Rachel are in *The Anchor*, book two in the *Haven of Rest* series.

God bless each one of you as you walk through this life. Keep your hand in His.

And the bit with Garnet's family appearing for a moment? That does really happen. My mother dropped dead in front of me, very unexpectedly. About six weeks after she graduated to heaven, I looked out of my bedroom window to see Mom standing and leaning against the fence around her garden. She looked well and happy and young. Her smile was just so precious to see once more. I glanced away and when I looked back, she was gone. I know that this was a God moment, that He had let me see Mom one last time.

Marrying quickly does happen. Mom and Dad were introduced in the fall before they married. They were then paired up by their minister to do visitation for the church. Ten weeks from the first time Dad walked Mom home, they married. They were engaged for 12 whole days. They had been married for fifty-six years when Mom graduated to heaven.

Ronna

www.ingramcontent.com/pod-product-compliance
Lightning Source LLC
Chambersburg PA
CBHW070344200726
48294CB00003B/783

9781998821358